John Payne

Songs of Life and Death

John Payne

Songs of Life and Death

ISBN/EAN: 9783744767385

Printed in Europe, USA, Canada, Australia, Japan

Cover: Foto ©Andreas Hilbeck / pixelio.de

More available books at **www.hansebooks.com**

SONGS

OF

LIFE AND DEATH.

SONGS
of
IFE AND DEATH

BY

JOHN PAYNE

AUTHOR OF

'INTAGLIOS : SONNETS,' 'THE MASQUE OF SHADOWS, ETC.'

'April that is me·senger to May'—CHAUCER

LONDON

HENRY S. KING & CO., 65 CORNHILL

1872

LONDON: PRINTED BY
SPOTTISWOODE AND CO., NEW-STREET SQUARE
AND PARLIAMENT STREET

DEDICATION

To Richard Wagner.

Master and chief of all for whom the singers
  Strain with full bosoms and ecstatic throats,
For whom the strings beneath the flying fingers,
  The clear pipes and the viols, yield their notes,—

Lord over all for whom the trumpets thunder,
  For whom the harps throb like the distant sea,
For whom the shrill sweet flutings cleave in sunder
  The surges of the strings that meet and flee,—

O strong sweet soul, whose life is as a mountain
  Hymned round about with stress of spirit-choirs,
Whose mighty song leaps sunward like a fountain,
  Reaching for lightnings from celestial fires,—

O burning heart and tender, highest, mildest,
　Nightingale-throated, with the eagle's wing,—
This sheaf of songs, culled where the ways are wildest
　And the shade deepest, to thy feet I bring!

I hail thee as from many hearts that cherish,
　Serve, and keep white thy thought within their shrines,
Where the flame' fades not, though its lustre perish,
　Midmost the lurid and the stormy signs.

I greet thee as from those great mates departed *
　Who first taught Song to know the ways of Soul,
Fit harbingers of thee, the eagle-hearted,
　Saw in the art the new sun-planets roll.

I greet thee with a promise and a cheering—
　I, that have loved thee many weary years,
I, that with eyes strained for the dawn's appearing,
　Have clung to thee for hope and healing tears;

I, that am nought, whose weakling voice has in it
　The shrill sole sadness of one wailing note;
No nightingale I, but a sad-voiced linnet,
　Piping thin ditties from a bleeding throat;

　　　　* Gluck, Schumann, Hector Berlioz.

I—since the masters lift no voice to-thee-ward
  To stay thy battle in the weary time—
Send forth for thee these weak-winged songs to seaward,
  To bear to thee their freight of idle rhyme.

Ah, how weak-voiced and little worth, my master!
  Yet haply, as a lark-song on the breeze,
That winging through the air, black with disaster,
  Heartens some exile pacing by the seas,

So even mine, my weak and unskilled singing
  May smite thine ear with no unpleasing notes,
What time the shrill sounds of the fight are ringing
  About thee, and the clamour of dull throats.

And peradventure (for least love is grateful)
  The humble song may, for a little while,
Smooth from thy brow the sadness high and fateful,
  Call to thy lips the rare and tender smile.

My harmonies are harmonies of sadness,
  My light is but as starlight on the wane:
Far nobler bards shall cheer thee with their gladness;
  I bring thee but the songpulse of my pain.

Be not disheartened, O our Zoroaster,
   O mage of our new music-world of fire !
Thou art not all unfriended, O my master !
   Let not the great heart fail thee for desire.

What matter though the storm-wind round thee rages,
   Though men judge weakly with imperfect sight !
O master-singer of the heroic ages,
   Each dawn is brighter with the appointed light.

Hate's echoes on the inconstant air but languish,
   Win not within the world's true heart to be,—
Faint wails for us of far-off souls in anguish,
   That chide their own sick selves in all they see.

Thine is the Future—hardly theirs the Present,
   The flowerless days that put forth leaf and die—
Theirs that lie steeped in idle days and pleasant,
   Letting the pageant of the years pass by.

For the days hasten when shall all adore thee,
   All at thy spring shall drink, and know it sweet ;
All the false temples shall fall down before thee,
   Ay—and the false gods crumble at thy feet.

Then shall men set thee in their holy places,
  Hymn thee with anthems of remembering ;
Faiths shall spring up and blossom in thy traces,
  Thick as the violets cluster round the spring.

And then, perchance, when in the brighter ages
  Men shall awake and know the god they scorned,
And, mad with grief, grave upon marble pages
  (*That therewithal the Future may be warned*)

The tale of their remorse and shame undying,
  They, coming where thy name has kept these sweet—
These idle songs of mine—shall set with sighing
  My name upon the marble at thy feet,

For that, when all made mock of and denied thee,
  Seeing not the portent and the fiery sword,
I from my dream in the mid-heaven descried thee,
  Saw and confessed thee, knew and named thee Lord.

CONTENTS.

What shall my song be of these latter days,

    These darkened days of toil and weariness?

Lo! for sheer burden of the grief that slays

    The adventure in men's hearts, and for the stress

Of doubt, my feet turn from the sunlit ways,

My eyes drink darkness from the morning rays,

    And my tongue curses where it fain would bless.

Ah! who shall cure the sickness of the time?

    Who shall bring healing to the wounded age?

Not I, forsooth. I—with my idle rhyme—

    Right gladly would I blazon all the page

Of life with flowers, and, with the happy chime

Of heart-free songs, lift up the folk to climb

    The peaks that soar out of the tempest's rage;

Ah, how soul-gladly!   But the life in me
*   Is worn with doubt and agony and care :*
Fain would I lead—alas ! I cannot see
*   Myself the way !   The presage in the air*
Weighs on my thought and will not set it free.
Ah God ! the helpless, saddened soul of me !
*   How shall I sing glad songs of my despair ?*

How shall I sing of aught but that I love ?
*   How should I be in love with aught but sleep ?*
I, that have watched the morning mists remove
*   And heaven break open to its grayest deep,*
Straining my eyes around me and above,
Only to see the dreams that erst I wove
*   Melt in the noonday, leaving me to weep !*

I, that thought once no ills should daunt my faith,
*   That hope should pluck the laurel from the abyss,*
Can this be I of old, this world-worn wraith
*   Of brighter days, living on memories*
And bitter food of dreams, in love with Death,
Seeking no laurel but a cypress-wreath,
*   Can this be I, with all my hopes grown this ?*

Alas! the long gray years have vanquished me,
  The shadow of the inexorable days!
I am grown sad and silent: for the sea
  Of Time has swallowed all my pleasant ways.
I am grown weary of the years that flee
And bring no light to set my bound hope free,
  No sun to fill the promise of old Mays.

For, let the summer throne it as it will,
  Life and the sun are sad and sere to him
(Sadder than Death and Night!) that wearies still
  For his delight, and sees upon the rim
Of the pale day no sign that shall fulfil
The covenant of promise every rill,
  Each flower swore to him, whilst the dawn broke dim.

How shall the sunlight thaw his wintry thought?
  His eyes gaze past the harvest and the throng
Of flower-crowned hours, to where the peace long sought
  Lies on the fields and all the stress life-long
Into the ice-calm woof of sleep is wrought:
Needs must he wander, with void hope distraught,
  Measuring his sad life with a less sad song.

SONGS

OF

LIFE AND DEATH.

———◦◦◦———

THE WESTWARD SAILING.

Oh, blithe and glad the liege-folk were
   In all the Norway strand !
For home the king a bride did bring—
   The king of all the land.

With many a gay gold flag they decked
   The city of the king ;
Loud sang the choirs, and from the spires
   The bells for joy did ring.

B

There was no man in all the land
But laid his grief aside,
What time the king with holy ring
Was wedded to his bride.

Within the royal banquet-hall
The bridal feast was spread ;
The cup went round, with garlands crowned,
And eke the wine ran red.

The harpers smote the silver strings,
The gleemen all did sing
Thereto a song so sweet and strong,
That all the hall did ring.

And therein sat upon his throne,
Among his barons all,
The king beside his trothplight bride,
And ruled the festival.

He kissed his bride, his bride kissed him,
　From the same cup drank they ;
And therewithal the minstrels all
　Did sing a joyous lay.

Oh, merry, merry went the feast,
　And fast the red wine ran !
The gates gaped wide, and in did stride
　An old seafaring man.

In russet leather was he clad,
　As those that use the sea,
And, three times rolled, a chain of gold
　About his neck had he.

Gray was his head, his beard was gray,
　And furrowed was his brow ;
But in his eye a might did lie
　That made all heads to bow.

He gazed upon the crownèd king,
    Upon the barons all ;
And there befel a sudden spell
    Of silence in the hall.

With steel-gray eyes he gazed on them,
    Whilst none the hush might break,
(The words to come were stricken dumb)
    And thus to them he spake :

' The lift is clear, the wind blows free
    Towards the sunset land ;
Oh, who with me will sail the sea
    Unto the Western strand ?

' Now let the courtier leave his feast,
    And plough the deep with me !
The king his bride let leave, to ride
    Over the briny sea !

' Now let the baron leave his hall,
    The minstrel leave his song !
 For in the West is set the quest
    Whereafter all men long.

'There are the forests thick with flower,
    And there the winds breàthe balm,
 And there gold birds sing wonder-words
    Under the summer calm.

' There is the earth thick strewn with gems,
    The sands are golden-shelled,
 And in the skies the magic lies
    That gives new youth to eld.

' Oh, who will sail the seas with me
    Unto the shores of gold ?
 There lieth rest, that is the best
    For all men, young or old.

Then up there leapt the crownèd king,
　　The king of all the land :
'Oh, I with thee will sail the sea
　　Unto the Western strand !

'Whate'er thou art, thy words have wrought
　　Such yearning in my breast,
That I will sail, come weal or bale,
　　Unto the golden West ! '

His bride hath laid upon his arm
　　Her hand more white than snow ;
She kissed him thrice, with tearful eyes,
　　And mouth all white for woe.

And on his finger, for a sign
　　That he should ne'er forget,
A ring threefold of good red gold
　　And sapphires hath she set.

The seaman led them with his hand
    Out of the high gold door ;
And they are come, for wonder dumb,
    Down to the white sea-shore.

Before the city, on the sea,
    A fair tall ship there lay,
With sails of silk as white as milk,
    And ropes of seagreen say.

Into the vessel tall and stout
    He led them every one ;
And as he bade, all sail they made
    Towards the setting sun.

Oh, many a weary day they sailed
    Across the silver spray !
And ever due the West wind blew, ·
    But never land saw they :

A wild wide waste of emerald sea,
  Flecked with the argent foam ;
A sun of gold that westward rolled
  Over the blue sky dome ;

The twilight gray, that ends the day,
  And then the moon on high ;
The purple night, with moonlight white,
  And stars thick set in sky.

So fifty days were wellnigh past,
  And on the fiftieth day,
At eventide, the sad wind sighed,
  The sapphire lift grew gray.

The icebergs rose around the ship,
  All in a death-white ring,
And grimly round with ice they bound
  The vessel of the king.

The helmsman stood beside the helm,
  The flesh from off him fell ;
And in his stead there was upsped
  A grisly Death from Hell.

The Death-King stood upon the deck,
  High as the topmost mast,
And thrice among that pallid throng
  He blew a deathly blast.

With the first breath the sky turned black,
  The sun a red fire grew,
And, ghastly pale, the hearts did fail
  Of all that luckless crew.

A second time he breathed on them
  Under the heavens' pall,
And with his breath the sleep of death
  Fell down upon them all.

A third time with his mouth he blew—
    His mouth without a lip—
And far below the chill tide-flow
    Down sank the doomèd ship.

Deep in the bosom of the sea
    The frozen Norsemen rest ;
Each mother's son the prize hath won
    That for all men is best.

All in the trance of that strange sleep,
    Upon the deck they stand ;
And Death the King, he hath the ring
    Upon his bony hand.

A SONG BEFORE THE GATES OF DEATH.[1]

Sed satis est jam posse mori.

I

SMITE strings, and fill the courts with thy lament !
Yea, let the singing thunder through the halls ;
Wake all the echoes from the funeral walls,
From aisle to roof, and porch to battlement !

Give forth thy sorrow till the roses' scent
Is blent for dole into the lilies' breath,
And all the air is faint with balms of death,
Seeing the glory of the day is spent,

---

[1] Suggested by Mr. Burne Jones' picture 'A Lament.'

And Death is very nigh upon our feet !
Sing out, and let the winds be filled with song !
   Haply, the clangours of the chant shall beat
Against the great gods' portals, till the throng ·
   Immortal hear in it the thunderous feet
Of Fate, and tremble for remembered wrong.

II

Give me the vase.   Drink deep as for the dead !
   Drink Life and all its joys a long good-bye !—
   Surely, the wine shall hearten us to die.

Blood of the grape !   Wine, that the earth has bled
From her slit painful veins, living and red
   With all the deaths that have won life for thee!
   I pour thee out for sign and memory,
For thanksgiving to life and goodlihead
   Of the green earth and all her kindly hours !
The homage of the dead, that in her sods

Shall soon lie low, and rot beneath the showers

Of the round year ; yet, when the kind Fate nods,

   Mayhap shall glorify the grass in flowers—

A godlike homage ! for the dead are gods.

III

The dead are gods ! seeing they lie and sleep,

   Folded within the mantle of the night,

     Ay, more than gods !   For lo, the heavy might

Of Death enrounds them!   Never do they weep,

Nor smile sad smiles, nor strain against the sweep

   Of rugged Doom.   There is no Fate for them,

     Lying, close-companied, within the hem

Of the pale fateful god : the long years creep

   Over their heads, and may not break their rest.

Who would not choose to die, when life is worn

   And wan with wrong unto the utterest ?

The fierce gods chase us to the brink with scorn ;

Yet smite the strings !   We are not so forlorn

   But we may die, seeing that death is best.

IV

Curse we the gods and die !   Give me the lyre.

Now, Zeus, fling thunders from thine armories !
And Helios, rain down sunbolts from thy skies !
We die and fear ye not, and all your ire,
Impotent as the flaming of a fire
Against the dead.   There is no hope for us,
Save of a sinking sweet and slumberous
Into the arms of rest.

Pile up the pyre !

Great father Zeus ! we reck not of thy grace !
It is thy wrath we crave with our last breath.
Look down in all thy terrors, King of Life !
Consume us with the splendours of thy face!
So shall the keen fire solve us like a knife,
And our sad souls be ravished unto death !

FALSE SPRING.

I

THE linnet tapped at the window-pane,
The hawthorn shook down its silver rain,
The flower-scents called me again and again :
  ' Come, for the spring is here ! '
O linnet ! the day is golden for thee ;
O hawthorn ! thy snow is pleasant to see ;
O flowers ! will the flower-scents waken for me
    The dreams that are dead and sere ?

' Come out, come out, O poet ! ' they said ;
' The violets wait in their cool green bed,
  The windflowers beckon with silver head,
    The pale blue crocuses linger

For thee, like a flame of the winter's end,
The hyacinth-clusters tinkle and bend,
The cowslips thrill with the scents they send
    To comfort the weary singer.

' The earth is singing her songs of green ;
The cuckoo pipes in the heart of the treen ;
There is no sadness in any, I ween,
    Under the new spring glamour.
Come out and live with the flowers again !
Thou hast fretted thy soul too long in vain
With the olden strife and the olden pain,
    And the weary worldly clamour.'

O breezes and birds ! I said, I fear
Ye should bring me again the past-time drear,
And the vanished shapes that I held so dear,
    With their tender tearful grace.
I fear ye should raise in the hawthorn-bowers
The sad sweet wraiths of the bygone hours,
And sadden my sight in the primrose-flowers
    With a dear dead maiden's face !

'O poet,' they said, 'the spring is glad;
The earth has buried the grief it had,
The fields have forgotten the winter sad,
 The woods are laughing with blossom :
There cometh no wraith of the bygone days
To moan in the wreaths of the woodbine maze;
But a golden glory of sunbeams plays
 Over the young land's bosom !'

O birds ! I fear ye will sing me anew
The golden songs that I taught to you,
When life was a kiss of the summer dew,
 Under the blossomed flowers !
O breezes ! I fear lest the voice of the dead
Should ring in your wafts, with the words she said.
And the silver rain of the tears she shed,
 In the old sweet happy hours !

'O poet !' they said, 'we will comfort thee,
No more shall our voices deceitful be ;
We will sing to thee songs of the things we see
 In the happy future's gold !

We will weave for thee delicate dreams and deep ;
We will vex thee no longer nor make thee weep ;
We will leave unstirred in their dreamless sleep
    The happy days of old ! '

II

There was no nay ; so out I went,
Under the apples blossom-sprent ;
    And the springtime kissed me, as I came,
    With blue-bell breath and crocus-flame ;
The birds did wreathe the air with singing,
And on the breeze there came a ringing,
    A noise of silver bells and gold,
    From out the woodlands, as of old.

My feet did turn towards the wood ;
And as I went, the hawthorns strewed
    White snow and rosy in my way,
    And throstles piped from every spray

There seemed no dole in aught, nor guile :
The happy earth was all a-smile
· With cowslip-gold and windflower-white ;
Spring held all things with its delight.

So to the forest's edge I came,
And saw the brooklet, like a flame
Of liquid silver, flow between
Lush column-work of arching green ;
Fair flowers laughed archly in the moss ;
The daffodils their heads did toss
For joyance ; and the gladsome bees
Hummed in the blue anemones.

There seemed no sadness in the air,
Nor any thought of things that were
For me of old, and are no more
Nor any of the sad old lore
That in my heart the years laid deep,
To lie and sleep a troubled sleep,
Did seem to stir in that sweet shade ;
And so I entered, undismayed. ·

III

O birds, 'twas not well done of you !
O flowers and breeze, right well ye knew
 The weary glamour that the spring
 Had laid for me on everything !
'Twas but to bring me back again
The memory of the olden pain,
 You lured me out, with songs of birds,
 With violet-breath and fair false words !

For lo ! my feet had hardly past
The woven band of flowerage, cast
 Betwixt the meadows and the trees,
 When, in the bird-songs and the breeze,
Another strain was taken up ;
And out of every blue-bell's cup
 The mocking voices sang again
 The olden songs of love and pain.

The flowers did mimic the old grace ;
The wan white windflowers wore her face ;
   And in the stream I heard her words ;
   Her voice came rippling from the birds.
Dead love, I saw thy form anew
Bend down among the violets blue,
   And, like a mist, the memory
   Of all the past came back to me.

IN ARMIDA'S GARDEN.

(Gluck's 'Armide,' Act ii. Scene 3.)

(Introduction and Aria.)

I

This is the land of dreams : these waving woods
    And the dim sunlight haze that hangs on all,
        And the clear jewels of the murmuring stream ;
    These flowered nooks through which the bird-notes
        fall,
Like silver spring-showers,—here sweet Silence broods,
    And here I dream.

Prone in the shadow of the flowers I lie,
    And watch the lizards glitter through the grass,
      And listen to the tinkle of the stream :
    Unmindful of the weary hours that pass,
Here do I lie and let the years go by :
      I dream and I dream.

Life and the world forsake me in the calm
    Of these enchanted woodways, green and still,
      Wherein the very sunlight's wavering gleam
    Sleeps on the lazy ripples of the rill,
And in the mist of the droopt flowers' faint balm
      I dream and I dream.

There is no future in these glades of ours,
    Nor any whisper of the stern to-morrow ;
      Life is a woven thing of a sunbeam :
    Nor in the grass is any snake of sorrow,
Nor comes remorse anigh where 'mid the flowers
      I dream and I dream.

Here are the bird-songs neither glad nor sad—
  Sleep drones in every note of their delight;
    Not even throstles with the olden theme
  Of tender grieving sadden the pale night;
But veiled is all their song, as 'twere they had
      Dream within dream.

Here are no roses of the sharp sweet scent,
  Nor the sad violets' enchanted breath,
    Nor jasmines cluster by the slumbering stream;
  But the drowsed hyacinths with umbels bent,
And the gold-hearted lilies of sweet death,
      Flowers of a dream.

I know not if life is with me, or how
  I come to lie and sleep away the years:
    I only know, but yesterday did seem
  Sad life amid a swarm of sordid fears
And hopes. Then came the god of Sleep—and now
      I dream and I dream.

II

There swell faint breaths to me of earthly jar,
   As 'twere a wild-bee humming in the thyme,
     And the dim sounds of what pale mortals deem
   The aims of life come back like olden rhyme
Upon my ears, whilst from the world afar
     I dream and I dream.

I hear the sweep of pinions in the air,
   And see dim glories glitter through the skies,
     As if some angel from the blue extreme
   Of heaven strewed gold and balm of memories
Upon the woods and the dim flowers that bear
     Spells of a dream.

There hover faces o'er me oftentimes
   Of lovely women that I knew of old,
     Set like a jewel in a golden stream
   Of fairest locks ; and from the aureoled
Sweet lips there swell faint echoes of old rhymes ;
     (I dream and I dream)

And sweet white arms enclose me as I lie,
  (Still do I lie and fold me in a sleep)
    And the soft fluttering tresses, all a-gleam,
  Fall down about my brow full tenderly,
And wind me in a glamour soft and deep.
      (*I dream and I dream.*)

Yet is there nothing that therein is rife,
  That for the world forsaken makes me sigh,
    Being but the empty motes of a sunbeam :
  Unheeding them, in the dim dream I lie ;
Far from the flutter of the wings of Life,
      I dream and I dream.

When wraiths of pleasure are so true and leal,
  Why should I seek for flesh and blood to love me ?
    Who shall tell what things are, and what things
      seem ?
  I am content, unquestioning, to feel
The folding of the shadow-arms above me.
      I dream and I dream.

III

There are two shapes that reign in the clear air,
  Filling the hours with their alternate feet :
    Under the lindens and along the stream
    The twin shapes walk and make the noonday sweet
With their clear songs and their aspèct most fair :
      (*I dream and I dream*)

The one of them is white and locked with gold,
  And the sea's blue is cloudless in his eyes;
    And therein comes and goes the glad sun's beam,
    When in the morn the sloping shadow lies
Of his fair form upon the golden wold:
      (*I dream and I dream*)

But dark the other is, and sad as night,
  And his eyes purple as the evening sky,
    When in the midnight falls the silver stream
    Of the pale moon upon the flowers that lie
And faint with the excess of their delight:
      (*I dream and I dream*)

The fair shape's songs are joyous as the day ;
   The other's sad as is the violet's breath ;
     And of their lovely semblance, this I deem,—
   Life is the name of him that is so gay ;
The name men know the other by is Death :
      (I dream and I dream)

The fair shape holds the day for his demesne,
   And wakes the linnets with his golden song,
     Clear as the jewelled tinkle of the stream ;
   The dark shape walks the cloistered night along,
And weaves descants of a divine sweet pain.
      (I dream and I dream.)

But in the middle day the twain do meet,
   And hand in hand right lovingly they go
     Along the flowered marges of the stream,
   Mingling their songs in a sweet chant and low ;
And where the grass is pressed by their twin feet,
      I dream and I dream.

Nor are these all that haunt the wooded bowers :
    There is another shape much sought of them,
      That something of the twain to have doth seem ;
    For there is life in his sweet eyes' blue gem,
And death upon his tender mouth's red flowers.
      (I dream and I dream.)

Walking alone, along the wood he goes,
    And plucks the flowers to breathe their scent and
      tell
    The issue of the things that he doth deem,
    And idles with the ripple's babbling swell,
Murmuring sweet ditties that he only knows.
      (I dream and I dream.)

Him do the twin shapes seek by hill and wood,
    He flying ever with an arch despite,
      Along the tangled borders of the stream ;
    And when upon the fringe of the spent night
The broidery of morning is renewed,
      (I dream and I dream)

They touch him often ; yet but seldom win
  To make him walk with them the path beside
    Along the woodways in the noontide gleam ;
  And often joyous Life hath grieving sighed,
And Death hath sorrowing sat beside the linn,
      (*I dream and I dream*)

For that he would not come : but, comes the wight,
  Then do they crown him, as their lord above
    The twain, with laurels and a diadem
  Woven out of sungold and the moon's delight ;
And so I know that the fair shape is Love.
      (*I dream and I dream.*)

These all are but the figures of a sleep,
  Being too fair for aught but the dream-world,
    Being too lovely to do aught but seem ;
  And so I will to lie, and them to reap :
In these dim hazes of the night impearled,
      I dream and I dream.

Come Death,—it is but night more sweet and deep ;

    Come Life,—it is but morning come again ;

      Come Love,—it is but the first spring's sun-gleam,

    With the sweet primrose-scents of rapturous pain ;

For Love, Life, Death, are but the terms of sleep.

      I dream and I dream.

HYMN TO THE NIGHT.

I

O NIGHT, that holdest all the keys of dreams,
Unfolding o'er the azure of the sea !
    I give thee welcome with a flowerful hand,
For lo ! I have been very fain for thee.
    I give thee loving welcome ! for meseems
Thou knowest well that I do love thee so,
        And in return dost hold my homage dear,
And lovest well to pour celestial balms
        Of comfort, that thy servant winds have fanned
Together, on me from thy cool dusk palms
            And from the jewelled hollow of thy sphere,
            Brimmed with moon-pearl and silver of the stars !

For often, when my heart was sore with scars
Of striving, and I could not weep for woe,
   Thine airs have brought sweet singings to mine ears
   And loosened all the silver springs of tears ;
Thy hands have soothed the fierceness from my grief,
   And in thy robe's wide purple thou hast drawn
   And folded all my sorrows, while the sills
Of heaven dropped sapphire. So I had relief
   Of sadness, ere the primrose of the Dawn
     Budded pale gold upon the emerald hills.

II

Thou knowest I have ever been to thee,
   Fair, simple Night, full constant in my love,
   How I have cherished, all delights above,
The folding of thy pinions over me.
   Mine has been no ephemeral fantasy,
That loves and loves not in one short hour's span,
   And knows not if Day's rose have sweeter breath
Than thine own violets ! Ere the noon began
   To burden all the air with weary gold

And doom all wandering winds to fiery death,

My spirit to thy sheltering arms did flee !

Ere yet the chariot of the sunset rolled

Fierce to the dying as an ancient knight,

And many a mist grew painted o'er the sea,

I saw thee in the haze, with silent feet

Sweep o'er the distance, Mother of the Night,

Wrapping the hills in shadow, fold on fold :

I saw thy vans across the landscape meet,

And my faint soul arose to welcome thee !

III

My faint soul sinks into thy windless deeps,

Misted with gold, O Mother of the Dreams !

And gazes with a wonderless content,

Up through thy lymph, to where the azure floors

Of heaven are with a gradual glory rent,

That through the cloisters of the æther leaps,

And in thy lap its spreading splendours pours,

In flood on flood of golden crested streams !

For slow sweet wonders lie for me impearled

Within thy womb and in thy jewelled sands ;

And all the lute-strings of my soul are swept,

By the unfolding ripples of thy tide

And rhythmic pulsing of thy tender hands,

To melodies of some enchanted world,

That through the ardour of the day has slept,

And will not glimmer through its veiling groves

Of tender mystery, till the Night divide

The gates of slumber ; songs of half-felt bliss,

And dreams through which a strange sweet echo roves,

And murmurs in a mist of fragrances,

And all sound's sweets do wane and swell and kiss,

Like night-birds in the blossomed oranges !

IV

My faint eyes loathe the ardours of the noon

And folded splendours of the dying sun ;

Joys that are stretched to madness, love that
burns,

And fierce delights that weary, scarce begun.

The roses wound me with their passionate bloom ;
   I weary of the lilies' laden breath ;
   And all the flowerage of my yearning turns¦
Towards its pearlèd lodestar of the moon,
   And waiteth for thy soft and kindly gloom,
O thronèd Night ! to soothe the hot fierce blue
   Of heaven with its webs of amethyst :
      My sad soul listens for thine airs to bring
      Soft harmonies and low to me, and sing
         Sweet songs of thee and of thy shadow Death !
And strains to see thy woven hands of mist
The meadows of the upper æther strew
With fair and tender lavishment of flowers,
   And sow thick goldcups in the purple meads,
   Far sweeter than the gay and flaunting weeds
That drink the sunlight in the noontide hours !

MADRIGAL TRISTE.

I

IF we should meet,

You and I,

My sweet,

In some fair land where under the blue sky

The scents of the fresh violets never die,

And Spring is deathless under deathless feet,

Should we clasp hands and kiss,

My sweet,

With the old bliss?

Would our eyes meet

With the same passionate frankness as of old,

When the fresh Spring was in the Summer's gold?

Ah, no ! my dear.

Woe's me ! our kisses are but frore ;

The blossoms of our early love are sere,

And will be fresh no more.

II

If we should stand,

You and I,

My sweet,

On that bright strand

Where day fades never, and the golden street

Rings to the music of the angels' feet,

Would our rent hearts find solace in the sky?

Should we lose heed,

My dear,

Of the sad years?

Would our souls cease to bleed

For the past anguish, and our eyes grow clear,

In heaven, from all the furrows of the tears?

Ah, no ! my dear.

Needs must we sigh and stand aloof !

Once riven,

God could not heal our love,

Even in heaven.

A SONG OF ROSES.

I

MANY a time and oft,
In the July weather,
When the breeze was soft,
And the pleasant land
Purple with the heather,
Went we hand in hand,
Love and I together.

Round our happy feet
Twinkled out the roses,
Roses red and sweet,
Ruddy as the sky
When the dawn uncloses,
White as chastity,
Yellow as primroses.

Were the roses red,

Lo ! my love was brighter !

Did the moonlight shed

Lilies on the ground,

Lo ! my love was whiter !

And her footsteps' sound

Than the breeze was lighter !

God ! how glad we were !

All the birds were jealous.

Hovering in the air,

All the larks and linnets,

All the white-breast swallows,

Envied all our minutes

More than they could tell us.

Thrushes knew no song

Like thy golden singing :

In the woodbirds' throng

There was no such sweetness
As thy voice's ringing
And thy footsteps' fleetness
O'er the heather springing.

Heavens ! how we kiss'd !
Flowers to one another
Bending through the mist
Of the summer-calm,
Kissing each his brother,
With their breath of balm,
Filled not one the other

With such golden bliss,
With such tender glory
Prisoned in a kiss ;
All the sweet spring-gladness,
All the summer-story
And the autumn-sadness,
When the sky is hoary.

II

Through the harebells blue
Went the bees a-humming,
Singing of the dew,
Of the summer ceas'd
And the harvest coming,
And the honey-feast
In the winter-gloaming.

Flower-dew, like the bee,
From thy lips of honey,
'Gainst the flower-time flee,
Stole I in Love's name,
While July was sunny,
That when winter came
I too might have honey.

Roses red and white
In my breast I treasured,
Whilst the sky was bright

And the fragrant ways
With the flowers were measured,
That in autumn's days
I might be rose-pleasured.

On my happy breast
Didst thou weep for gladness ;
And thy tears, out prest,
Falling on the roses,
Filled them with strange sadness,
Sweet as birdsong-closes,
In the new May-madness.

Then I learnt the song
That thy lips did utter ;
Caught the jewelled throng,
Every glad clear trill,
Every low sweet mutter,
At thy voice's will
That did fly and flutter ;

Treasured every note
In my heart's recesses,
Learnt them all by rote,
All the golden falls,
All the silver stresses,
All the joy that thralls,
All the love that blesses ;

Stored them dearly up
In the hidden places,
In the white closed cup
Of my flower-bell fancies;
That, when white earth's face is,
And the old romances
Gone with summer's graces,

When my soul should grope
In the earth-mists sordid,
Far from love and hope,

I might turn for balm
To the music hoarded,
And in its sweet psalm
Hope and be rewarded.

III

So the summer fled,
And the autumn mellowed
All the leaves to red,
All the corn to gold;
And the winter followed
With its silent cold
And its snows wind-hollowed.

Then I went alone ;
For light Love had left me
When the birds had flown
And the flowers were dead :

Winter had bereft me
Of the roses red
And the bliss Love weft me.

Then I said, ' Have heart !
Thou hast yet thy treasure.
Though light Love depart,
Thou canst summon up
All the summer leisure,
From its silver cup,
All the bygone pleasure.'

So I searched my heart
For the hoarded sweetness,
Honey set apart
For the days of sadness ;
For the songs whose fleetness
Gave the summer gladness,
Gave my bliss completeness.

Lo ! the songs were wails,
Like the wind that surges
Through the moaning sails !
Lo ! the sweets were gall !
Lo! the thoughts were scourges ▸
Bitter honey all ;
And the songs were dirges !

Then from out my breast
Did I take the roses,
Roses tear-caress'd,
Roses red and white,
That in the reposes
Of the noon-delight
I had plucked for posies.

Lo ! the flowers were dead,
By the frost invaded ;
But the tears she shed

Had within the fronds
Of the petals shaded,
Grown to diamonds,
Lights that never faded.

So Love's gladness flees,
And its sweets turn bitter ;
But the memories
Of its hours of sorrow,
Holier and fitter,
In the winter morrow,
Turn to gems and glitter.

THE BALLAD OF THE KING'S DAUGHTER.

I

THE night-wind wails,
The moon-silver pales,
The stars are faint in the mist;
The king's daughter rides over hill and dale,
Under the arch of the pine-shade pale,
A lily of gold in the moon-mist's veil.
And as she rides
Where the mill-stream glides,
A raven is sitting on the tree by the brown water,
With '*Woe to thee! oh, woe to thee, king's daughter!
Thou ridest to an evil tryst!*'

The silence quivers,

The pine-shade shivers,

Sad flute-notes wake in the gloom.

The king's daughter rides in the hawthorn track ;

Gold is her hair on the black steed's back.

Whose steps are those

That the echo throws

Back on the startled ear of the night ?

What form is that in the moonlight white

That follows the track of her horse's feet ?

Whose hands on the red-gold bridle meet ?

Whose spells are they that such ills have wrought her,

That the night-winds cry to her, ' *Woe, king's daughter !*

Thou ridest to thy place of doom !'

The moon brims up

In her pearlèd cup,

The air grows purple as gore ;

The stars are red

With blood to be shed ;

2

The king's daughter sees in the purple sky
The wings of the birds of ill omen fly,
And the broidered lights in the cloud-rack burn
With a word that is weary and fierce and stern ;
The shadows of the night in their arms have caught her;
And the night-winds cry to her, ' *Woe, king's daughter !*
For thy pleasant place of life shall never know thee
     more !'

        Out of the maze
        Of the woodbind ways,
        Into a moonlit glade,
    The maiden rides, with the shape of gloom
    Casting a shade on her cheek's rose-bloom,
    With a feeling of swiftly hastening doom.
What glitter is that of silvered mail,
Prone on the grass in the moonlight pale ?
        A sword-hilt joined to a broken blade :
    Whose blood is red on the bright brown steel ?
        Who lies in the sleep of death ?
    It is her knight, that was true and leal,

Whose lips so often her lips have kiss'd,

To whom the shades of the night have brought her !

And she hears in the echo his dying breath :

  ' Ah ! woe is me for thee, king's daughter !

    Thou comest to a woful tryst !'

II

She hath alighted from off her steed,

  And she hath raised her lover's head,

    And laid it on her knee ;

-The rose of her heart begins to bleed,

  And on her hair his blood is red ;

    Her heart begins to freeze.

She hath arisen from off the ground,

  And she hath ta'en the bloodied blade,

    And dug with it a grave ;

She hath diggèd a grave both deep and round,

  And there his body hath she laid :

    His soul the dear Christ save !

She hath folded her round her mantle gray,
   And she hath stepped into the tomb,
     And laid her by his side :
The dead and the live, the knight and his may,
   They are wedded at last in night and gloom :
     The grave is fair and wide.

III

The day-flower blows on the eastern hills.
   (Woe is me for the king's daughter !)
     The throstle in the morn
     Sings blithely on the thorn,
And golden is the sun on the grave of the king's
daughter.

The wind of dawn through the forest shrills,
   With leaves for the grave of the king's daughter.
     A lily of red gold
     Its flower-flames doth unfold,
And glisters in the sun from the heart of the king's
daughter.

A FAREWELL.[1]

I

To part in midmost summer of our love,
    When first the flower-scents and the linnet's tune
    Have fallen into harmonies of June
About our lives new linked, and all above
    The flower-blue heaven lies for bliss aswoon,—
Were this not sad? .Yet love must live by pain,
If one would win its fragrance to remain.

II

Were it not sadder, in the years to come,
    To feel the hand-clasp slacken for long use,
    The untuned heartstrings for long stress refuse
To yield old harmonies, the songs grow dumb
    For weariness, and all the old spells lose
The first enchantment?   Yet this thing must be.
Love is but mortal, save in memory.

[1] Suggested by a sketch by Mr. Simeon Solomon, entitled 'The Parting.'

III

Too rare a flower it is, its bloom to keep
  In the raw cold of our unlovely clime,
  Too frail to thrive in this our weary time.
I would not have thy kisses, sweet, grow cheap,
  Nor thy dear looks round out an idle rhyme,—
And so I hold that we loose hands and part ;
Dear, with my hand you do not loose my heart.

IV

Sweet is the fragrance of remembered love ;
  The memory of clasped hands is very sweet,
  Joined lips that did not once too often meet,
And never knew that saddest word ' Enough !
  And so 'tis well that, ere our springtime fleet,
Thus in the heyday of our love part we :
Farewell, and all white omens go with thee !

v

Is it not well that we should both retain
 The early bloom of love, untouched and pure ?
 There is no way by which it may endure,
Save if we part before its sweetness wane
 And wither ; since that life is so impure,
And love so frail, it may not blossom long,
Unscathed, amid our stress of care and wrong.

vi

We were not sure of love, my sweet,—and yet
 The fragrance of its Spring shall never die.
 Sweetheart, we shall be sure of memory,
That amber of the years, where Time doth set
 The dear-belovèd shapes of things gone by,
Whereby their gentle semblance may evade
The ills that lurk in eld's ungenial shade.

VII

So, sweet, our love shall, in the death of it,
　　Revive, as corn that withers in the ground,
　　And somewhile after casts fresh blades around
And yields full golden sheavage, as is fit.
　　It may be that new flowers will too be found
Among the stubble, and the pale sweet blooms
Of Autumn glorify our woodland glooms.

VIII

The memory of our kisses shall survive,
　　And in the glass of time be consecrate.
　　Our love shall with the distance grow more great,
And shall for us be sweeter than alive,
　　When dead ; for memory shall reduplicate
The sweetness of the past, till you and I
Cherish as angels' food each bygone sigh.

THE WIND OF THE WESTERN WATER.

I

A WIND came over the Western water,
(*Oh sweet is the rose in the fresh Spring-time !*)
' Weary of life,' it said, ' poor lover?
   Sick for a love that is dead and gone?
(Winds blow over her, earth's above her.)
   Sick for a day that was faded at dawn ?
The cure is the kiss of the marsh-king's daughter.'

   Weary of life, I answered and said,
      (O wind of the Western water !)
   Sick for a day and a love that are dead,
   ' Why should I seek,' I answered and said,
      ' For the kiss of the marsh-king's daughter ? '

II

The wind came over the Western water :

    (*The death-flower blows in the Summer's prime !*)

' If one be weary and sick of living,

    Sick for the sake of a vanished love,

        Sick of the glow and blossom of Spring,

        Sick of the Summer's glitter and ring ;

If colour lack in the Autumn's weaving,

    And the Winter hold not sorrow enough,

The cure is the kiss of the marsh-king's daughter ! '

Weary of life, I answered and said,

    (O wind of the Western water !)

Bitter with tears that I could not shed,

' Tell me, Westwind,' I answered and said,

    ' The home of the marsh-king's daughter ! '

III

' It lies far over the Western water,

    (*Oh sweet is the rose in the fresh Spring-time !*)

Under the arch of the sun at setting,
   'Twixt gold of sunset and dusk of night,
Under the sound of the seawind's fretting ;
     In the purple heart of the marish mist,
     That the shafts of the dying day have kiss'd,
Under the ceiling where stars are bright,
There is the home of the marsh-king's daughter.'

Weary of life, I answered and said,
   (O wind of the Western water !)
· 'My hopes lie close in the house of the dead ;
But I will go,' I answered and said,
   ' To seek for the marsh-king's daughter.'

'

IV

I wandered over the Western water,
   (*Oh sweet is the rose in the fresh Spring-time !*)
And I came in the evening, when light was dying,
   To a land where the hum of the world was still,
And the voice of the evening wind was sighing,

And the spells of sleep were over the air ;
And I saw in the setting the golden hair
Of the sunset broider the mists, until
They grew to the robe of the marsh-king's daughter

Golden starlets were over her head,
(A crown for the marsh-king's daughter).
' Come to my arms,' I answered and said ;
And she came, with the Westwind's murmurous tread,
To me that so long had sought her.

V

A voice came over the Western water :
(*The deathflower blows in the Summer's prime !*)
' Dearly,' it said, ' hast thou won and bought her.
Her kisses are cold as are the dead,
And the gold of her hair o'er thee is shed
As wings of the birds that fly to the slaughter !
The lips thou shouldst kiss are living and red,

Thine eyes should feast on the joys of earth,

    Thy hands pluck flowers in the golden prime.

Youth was not made for sorrow and dearth :

    Get thee back, whilst there yet is time ;

For Death is the name of the marsh-king's daughter!'

    Weary of life, I answered and said,

        (O wind of the Western water !)

    'My lips shall kiss but the lips of the dead.'

    Sick of the day, I answered and said,

        ' Kiss me, O marsh-king's daughter !

AUBADE.

I

When the flocks of the morning gather in the East,
    Golden fleeced,
And the star-sparkles of the night are drawn
Into one great orient pearl of dawn,
    The voice of my soul is as a bird that mourns
      Because the night has ceased !
My voice is as a sorrowful sweet singing,
    That murmurs o'er dim notes of faded morns
Thick-misted with pale memories round them
    clinging,
    Whose faint fresh bud of dawning did unfold
    Into the noonday's burning flower of gold ;
And all the cloisters of the air are ringing

With dreams of things that have been done and
told
For me in days of old.

II

Amber of dawn, thou bringest me scant pleasure !
Sad treasure
Of fair and precious jewels that the years
Have worn and dulled with bitter rills of tears.
Thy gold is as the wraith of bygone hope
Poured without measure
Upon the upland meadows of my youth,
When Edens glittered on each cloudward slope,
And all the sweet old lies seemed fairest sooth,
When all things wore the tender glow of dreaming !
(Alas ! that such sweet error should have blown
To seeding, and such bitter fruit have sown !)
Ah me ! meseems the halls of heaven are streaming
With many a sweet old memory that has flown
And left me sad and lone.

F

III

Time was, the dawnflower on the hills unfolding,
  To me, beholding,
Brought visions of a fair and far ideal,
And seemed the chalice of a new Sangreal!
  I dreamt that I might win life's balm, and bid
   My fellows to the holding
Of the banquet of a new and nobler being,
  Wherefrom old glooms and horrors should be rid,
And no one eye should be shut out from seeing;
  Where the despairing soul of man, grown faithful
  To its own self, should find life no more scathful
With weary doubt and thrice accursèd ease,
  And the enfranchised air no more be wraithful
With phantoms of time-honoured wrong, that freeze
   The speech in him that sees,—

IV

Sees, and is sick to vent his soul in singing,
  That the song, ringing

Athwart the wild waste beauty of the world,

May free it from the dragons that lie curled

    Round its sad heart; back to the glory golden

        Of old, Earth's deserts bringing !—

And may not work his will for damnèd use.

    I dreamt that I might bring the unbeholden

Fear, that doth steep with such a venomed juice

    The cup of being, to the light of dawn,

    And show it powerless—and, that curse withdrawn,

Life should bloom fresh and fair with healthful dews.

    This was my dream, O amber of the dawn,

        In days long since bygone.

V

Lo, I have fought and perished in the striving !

        Lo ! and arriving

Before my goal of crystal and of gold,

Have seen its glories shrink off, fold by fold,

    Leaving the bare waste hopelessness exposed !

        I have grown sick with riving,

F 2

Mist after mist, the opals of the mirage,
   That for my sight, blinded with dreams, enclosed
The prize of some new hero-high aspirage,
   Gold to be won by who should dare the winning,
   Who should cast off and leave in the beginning
The cumber of the fatal Past's empirage,
   And to old signs a new rich meaning giving,
      Through death and sin win living !

VI

Lo, I have failed and fallen in the gaining !
     In the attaining
Life, has Death entered deep into my soul !'
Lo, I have sunk defeated at the goal !
   Eos, thy banners of the triumph, streaming
      Over the pale night's waning,
Are wraiths to me of old deceptive glory,
   Gold of the victory of the darkness, gleaming
Over the hills with pennants red and gory !
   For me, thy downward heaven-reddening flood
   Is as the river of the flush of blood

That hearts of men have shed for thy false story,

Since day first glittered on the new-born world,

Sun-crowned and iris-pearled !

VII

Long to my sight the night has been the fairer,

The bearer

Of comfort to the souls of those that languish

With hopeless hope and weary with the anguish

Of saddening joy : the glamour of the setting

Sweeter and rarer,—

In the faint sadness of its purple fading

Towards the silver night and her forgetting,

Where there is only balm and no upbraiding,—

Is to my soul, that wearies for reposing,

More grateful than dawn-daphne's fierce unclosing,

Wherein for aye I see old hopes evading

My grasp, and with a mocking light regilded,

Waste dreams my young hands builded !

COURANTE.

I

SILVER Spring,

Hawthorn-white,

Violet-scent,

May-delight ;

Birds that sing

Noon and night,

Meadows sprent

With sunlight ;

Woods that ring

With the pent

Streams that twine

In their flight

Shade and shine :

Whose content
Do they bring?
Whose delight?
Ah, not mine!

II

Gold of June,
Days on fire
With flower-flush
Of desire :
Sun-sprent noon,
Hedge and brier
Rose a-blush
High and higher;
Linnet's tune,
Trill of thrush,
Nightingales
In the hush
Of the moon :

What avails
All the flush
Of the grass,
All the rush
Of the hours
That o'erpass
Earth and sea,
Crowned with flowers,
Unto me?
What? alas!

III

Light of Love,
Lips that cling,
Hands that meet,
Souls that wing
Heavens above,
Wandering,
Joined and sweet;
Thoughts that sing,

Lives that move
To the beat
Of the hours,
Murmuring,
' Heaven is ours,
Ours that love,
While we twine,
Hand in hand
In the shine
Of Love's land ; '
Whose glad feet
Tread that strand,
All divine,
Whose blest hand
Gathers flowers
In Love's land?
Ah, not mine !

IV

Who complains?
Ah, not I !

Not a tear, .
Not a cry!
All the rains
Of the sky
Cannot clear
Souls that sigh
Of their stains :
But I lie,
Many a year,
Grief-opprest,
And the pains
In my breast,
Never rest,
Never die.

THE DEAD MASTER.

A Threnody.

Quis desiderio sit pudor aut modus
Tam cari capitis?

I

WERT thou not with us, when the night departed,

O strong sweet singer that art ours no more !

Was not the harping thine that first gave o'er

The song of wailing, when the daybreak parted,

And the glad heavens broke open, shore from shore,

Sun-crowned and iris-hearted?

II

Didst thou not smite the strings to jubilation,

Hymning the grand sweet scope of the To be?

Did not our midnight dole and doubting flee

From thy glad strength, and all our lamentation
  Swell with thy song into an ecstasy
    Of aspiration?

III

No more we wept and wailed for Life's undoing,
    Following the golden notes that brake from thee,
    Riding star-crowned upon that sudden sea
That from thy soul poured forth for our renewing
    Oceans of hope and jubilance, that we
        Drank in, ensuing.

IV

Didst thou not rend for us the gloom descending,
    Scatter the veils of doubting from our sight,
    Bring to our lives again the flower-delight,
Bird-songs and field-scents in thy verses blending?
    Didst thou not save our spirits from the night
        Stern and impending?

V

Lo ! and the night has bound thee, O our master !
 Lo ! and the shadows gather round thy place !
 Shall we then no more look upon thy face?
Surely the shades will fold to night the faster,
 Surely Death's torches quicklier replace
  Life's lamp of alabaster !

VI

Shall we then no more see thee, O our singer,
 Passing the love of women to our souls?
 Shall then our lives be darkened and our goals
Deep in the gray dim distance fade and linger,
 Since that no more thy voice our steps controls,
  No more thy finger

VII

Points and is clear along the hills that darken,
 Clear with the distant glimmer of the day?
 Will then the cliff-walls never roll away,

That thy song's sweetness hide from us that hearken,

    Us that are weary in Life's mazèd way,

        Weary of mists that starken ?

VIII

Have we then heard thy singing for the last time

    Shape us the glories of the olden days ?

    Have we a last time listened to the lays,

Wherein thou scal'dst the ancient heavens for pastime

    And in the future's iridescent haze

        Buildedst the past-time ?

IX

Can we forget thee, high sweet soul and faithful,

    Homer and Pindar of our modern time,

    Lord of our thought and leader of our rhyme,

Thou that didst clear the air that was so deathful,

    Filled it anew with scents of rose and thyme,

        Made it bird-breathful ?

X

Thou that for us wert some sublime Silenus,
  Full to the lips of wise and lovely words,
  Shaping to song the speech of flowers and birds,
Wert as a god on whose strength we might lean us,
  And, our Apollo, piped to us thy herds
    Songs of Camœnus !

XI

What does it matter if we never saw thee,
  Knew but thy presence as a god's afar,
  Heard but thy song as music of a star ?
Were we not with thee, part in thee and of thee?
  Were not our souls akin to thine and are ?
    Did we not love thee ?

XII

With thee we lived in some enchanted Arden,
  Glad with the echo of the wood-nymphs' feet,
  Bright with old memories, very strange and sweet,

That in the shade of that Armida's garden
    Did from our cold pale daylight hide and fleet,
        Where all things harden.

XIII

Thou wast no wailer, no sweet-voiced unmanner,
    That for weak men within an idle clime
    Builded vain dreams to sweet and idle rhyme :
Thou hast built souls after the antique manner,
    Souls that shall march through many a lapse of time,
        Bearing thy banner,

XIV

Thy standard with its burden high and golden,
    Daring to love, and loving know no shame,
    Wit to reject the let of age-old blame,
Faith to rekindle altar-ashes olden,
    Fan the old love of Nature to full flame,
        Long unbeholden !

XV

Friend, we have mourned and longed for thee with
mourning;
Poet, our ears are sad with listening,
Straining for songs no breeze shall ever bring ;
Master, thy lapse has dulled with dusk Life's morning,
Scathed with black death each bright and lovely
thing,
That in the adorning

XVI

Of thy high verse has erst been wont to sparkle,
Glitter and glow with glories of the past ;
Spirit of song and flame of faith, the blast
Of thine eclipse has reft from us, anarchal,
Robbed us with thee of all the things thou wast,
Bard patriarchal !

XVII

Master, in vain we listen for thy singing,
Listen and long and languish for desire !

G

Unto our ears no echoes of thy lyre

Pulse from the darkness, no glad breeze comes bring-

    ing

    Voices, no sparkles of the ancient fire

        Reach us, wide-winging !

XVIII

Will then thy song no more translate our yearning,

    Mould our harsh cries to music of the spheres ?

    Will thy verse glitter no more with our tears ?

Has then the sun of thy bright soul, whose burning

    Lightened so oft the midnight of our fears,

        Set, unreturning ?

XIX

Or hast thou found thy dream in plains supernal,

    Shapes of fair women, forms of noble men,

    That at the magic summons of thy pen

Did from the snows and solitude hybernal

    Where they so long had slept, seek out again

        The meadows vernal ?

XX

Do the long lapses of the ghost-land, lying
    Stretched out beyond the·portals of the grave,
    Teem with fresh fruits and flowers for thee and wave
With the clear shapes of thine old dreams undying?
    Has the dark flood been powerful to lave
      From thy soul, sighing

XXI

Grief and the very memory of grieving,
    Hope and the very thought of wearying
    After the glow and glory thou didst sing?
Hast in the air such unimagined giving,
    Splendour and flush of every godlike thing,
      Wherefor thy living ·

XXII

Struggled and wearied in the bitter days?
    Dost thou live out thy phantasies of gold
    Under Greek skies and Attic woods of old,

G 2

Walk, crowned with myrtle, in the Dorian ways,
  Peopled with all the dreams that did unfold
    In thy high lays?

XXIII

Surely this thing alone could hold thee speechless,
  Surely in this alone couldst thou forget
  Us that are left to struggle in the net
Of the sad world, to feel the days grow each less
  Sweet to our souls, to weary with the fret,
    Dumb and beseechless.

XXIV

Surely thy soul would yearn to us with longing!
  Surely, no grave could keep thy voice from us,
  Were not this so! The silence dolorous
Surely is voiceful of the years prolonging
  Long bliss for thee and us to come, that thus
    Unto the thronging,

XXV

Unto the cry and clamour of our yearning,
  Still is the air and stirless is the light,
  That from the grey grim bosom of the night
Comes back no sign or voice of thy returning,
  Echoes no memory of the old delight,
      Weariness spurning !

XXVI

Well, be it so ; mayhap, some day, unknowing,
  We too may rest and come to where thou art,
  Press thee again full-raptured to our heart,
Gaze in thine eyes with eyes no less fire-glowing,
  And in like bliss forget the olden smart,
      The weary going

XXVII

Friendless and dumb across the ways of being,
  Cast off the memory of the years we sighed
  After thy song and presence sunny-eyed,

In the new splendour of thy lays, the seeing
　All the old hopes fulfilled and sanctified,
　　No longer fleeing

XXVIII

Mirage-like from us through the earthly hazes,
　Haply we too shall leave our olden pains
　Off with our life and all its weary stains,
Put on like joy amid the light that blazes,
　And the glad day that floods those golden plains,
　　Those songful mazes !

XXIX

Till then, farewell !—the joy shall be the greater
　When we clasp hands and hearts to part no more :
　For that the long lone life has been so sore,
For that no sign of thee to death played traitor,
　Sharper shall be the bliss for us in store,
　　Sweeter if later.

A PARABLE.

I

A POEM is a painted window-pane.

If one looks into churches from the street,

All dark and gloomy seems the holy shrine;

And so at poems looks the Philistine;

Thus may he well with disappointment meet,

And out of humour all his life remain.

II

But only come into the dark inside,

And greet the fair interior of the shrine.

At once, it will with brightest colour shine;

A jewelled light will through the windows glide.

And pictures from the dull blotched tints combine,

That will God's chosen children edify,

And with unfailing beauty charm the eye.

From Goethe.

INTO THE ENCHANTED LAND.

I

WHEN the end of the enchantment of the Summer is
  at hand,
   In the month that closes
    The blue Midsummer weather,
   When the passionate red roses
     Faint for the heat
    And the lilies fold together
     Their petals pale and sweet,—
  In the burning noontide hazes
  And the golden glory of the flowers that blazes
   Over the happy valleys and the wold,
There swells to me a breeze ofttimes
   Out of the dreams of old.

And in the breeze the murmur of old rhymes

  Rises and falls

  Like some enchanted singing,

 And my tired brow is fanned

   By odours from the halls

Of dreamland, such as in the moonlight white

Float round a wandering knight,

When thro' the country of the elves he fares

 And wonders at the dances

 That glitter through the moonglow, and the ringing

  Of elfin bells ;

And through the fluttering of the frolic airs,

  In all the song there swells

A voice well known to me of bygone days,

 That calls me to forsake

The weary worldly ways,

And as of olden times my way to take

 Into the dreamland of the old romances,

  Into the enchanted land !

II

Down falls the evening on the weary plains,

And I, I stand and wait

Where, at the verge

Of the green fields, the stains

Of sunlight fade upon the trees that surge

Out of the falling night,

Dim as the dreamland's gate.

And so there comes to me a flash of light

Across the shadow, and my faint eyes know

The robe of her I love,

And the bright crown of tresses aureoled

Star-glorious above

Her face's rosy snow,

Spangling the shades with gold.

' Ay, love ! sweet welcome ! I had need of thee,

Sore, sorest need ! '

Still doth she grow

Nearer and lovelier till my arms may press

Almost her charms and all my soul may feed
    Upon her loveliness.
     But lo ! I clasp the wind,
     And in mine arms entwined
Is nothing but a fair and painted dream !
' Dear love, why dost thou seem
    And torture me with hope in vain?'
     And the fair shape doth weep,
   And comforts me again
    With lovely looks and words of amity ;
     And so my pain doth sleep
   And there is peace once more for me !

III

'Come, love,' she saith, 'the dream-gates gape for thee !
    The hour of glamorous delight
  Is come for thee and me !
    Under the silver night
     We shall walk hand in hand
    In the enchanted land,

And see the moon-flowers blossom to the sound '
    Of the sweet elfin tune,
        As in the days gone by.
Dost thou not hear the horns of Faërie wound
    Among the elfland bowers,
And all the rush of splendid song that floods
    The silver winds that lie
And idle in the pearl-work of the moon,
    Woven about the woods ?
Come, love ! the day is dead,
    With all its weary hours,
    And ours in newly born !
Thou shalt have easance of thy woes this night
    Amid the glory of the flowers that swoon
        With magical delight,
Ere in the sky creeps up the weary morn,
    And the pale East grows red !'

IV

So in the pale faint flush of the twilight,
    Softly I ope the door,

And hand in hand

Across the fields we go, before

The day has parted from the night,

Among the cloisters where the tall trees stand,

White in the woodland ways

Under the moonlight, till a wall of mist

Rises before us in the evening haze,

Silver and amethyst.

Then doth my love loose hands,

And in the spangled green

Of the thick moss she stands

Within the wood-verge, where the sun has been

And is not faded quite ;

And to the hovering night

Sweet mystic lays

And songs she singeth, very pure and high,

Until there answereth

From out the heart-green of the woodbine maze

A magic singing, as it were

A woven music of the scents that lie

In all the night-flowers' breath;
And with the song upon the fragrant air
Strange mystic memories do swell and die
Of Love and Life and Death.

v

The gate of dreamland opens to the singing,
And hand in hand we go,
My love and I,
Along the woodways with the elfsongs ringing,
Under the silver night,—
And down the vistas of the trees, that lie
And bathe in the moonlight,
There swells to us a murmur sweet and low,
As of some magic river,
That glitters through its ranks of waving reeds
And makes the flower-bells quiver
With haunting melodies;
And from its ferny nest
The runnel of a brooklet sings and speeds

Across the pearlèd network of the grass,

　Murmuring its loveliest,

　　Songs of a heart at ease,

　That in its joy doth pass

　　Into a tune ; and lo !

Upon the diamond ripples to our feet

　A little shallop floats,

　　Out of a rush-work woven all and wrought

　　With pearls and ivory.

　　Then in the skiff do we

Embark and down the silver stream we fleet,

　　Under the thronging notes

　　　Of the night-birds ;

　　　And as we go,

The air is all astir with lovely things ;

　Sweet music, twinned and fair with magic words,

　　Rises from elfin throats,

　And in the leaves we see the rush and glow

　　Of jewelled wings.

VI

There lies all glamour in the arching banks,

Through which our river runs :

Over us wing the dreams,

And in the pale sweet trances of the moon,

Along the stretching glades,

The silver fawns of Faërie do pass,

White in the sweet white beams ;

And now and then the tune

Of horns is clear,

And the elf-hunt sweeps by with glittering ranks

Across the velvet grass :

The king's tall knightly sons

Ride through the aisles, with many a douçepere ;

And now there comes a throng

Of snow-white maids,

Gold-haired,

That with sweet song

And pleasance wander in the fragrant maze

Of the cool woodland ways,

Sweet one with sweet one paired,

All through the summer night,
And win the enchanted air
Into melodious trances with the ring
Of their flute-voices and the fair delight
Of their gold-rippled hair,
Soft as the songs they sing.

VII

The high trees bend above us lovingly,
As on the stream we go,
Mingling their boughs above
Into a flower-starred roof
Of lovely greenery ;
And through the night
The fireflies glow
And glitter, as it were
The stars had left their places for delight,
And through the woodland air
Sped singing.
The stream makes music to the cleaving prow,

Answering the birds' descant

And the soft ringing

Of bindweed bells.

The night is filled with spells

Of old delight ;

The summer air is hazed and jubilant

With ripples of the glory of song gold

And elfin blisses ;

And, in the lovely light,

A maiden more than earthly fair to see,

With moon-webs aureoled,

My lady sits by me,

Answering my thought with kisses.

VIII

The river shallows through the grass and flowers

Along the waning night ;

And now the boat is gone

From underneath our feet ;

And eke the stream has faded

Into the ripple of the white moonlight ;

And in the midwood bowers

We stand alone

In the still time and sweet

Before the hour when night and morning meet.

Sweet sooth, the moon has braided

The air to pearl,

And down the haunted glades

The shadows dance and whirl

Among the sheeny hosts of the grass-blades,

In the cool glitter of the time :

And lo ! my thought takes rhythm from their dances,

And to my lips comes rhyme,

And many a lovely tune,

Such as the minstrels of the old romances

Sang to the moon.

IX

So rings my singing through the elfland aisles,

Waking the silver bells,

That lie and dream in the flower-sleep,

Deep in the mossy dells ;

H 2

And as I sing,

The timid rabbits creep

From all their soft warm nests among the fern,

And in the wood-deeps gold and silver strewn,

The fawns stand listening.

Then down the columned way,

Through which the moonlight smiles,

There rings the trample of a horse's feet.

Nearer it grows along the ripple-play

Beside the tinkling burn,

Until the silver armour of a knight

Shines in the moon,

And a clear voice trolls songs of war and love,

Ditties of strange and mystical delight,

That through the trees do rove,

Singing of Day and Night,

Of Love and Life and Death,

With strains as bright and sweet

As is the linnet's breath.

X

My weak song ceases as I look on him :
'Fair knight,
Fair minstrel, teach me all thy might.
I know thee as of old.
Clear through the twilight of the legends dim
Thy name like gold
Doth shine,
And the fair nobleness of thy white life
Sweetens the lips of men,
O Percivale, Christ's knight ! '
And then he gazes on me with mild eyes,
And the clear rapture floods me like a wine
Of some old Orient tale,
Purging my heart from sighs
And memories of strife.
And so he rides into the gloaming pale,
Scattering on every hand
Sweet singings, till they die upon the ear.
Then, looking round again,

I see the night has ceased,

And in the dawning drear

My dream fades from me, as the skies are spanned

By the red bars of morn,

And in the East

The cold gray day is born.

VOCATION SONG.

'La poésie est semblable à l'amandier: ses fleurs sont par-
fumées et ses fruits sont amers.'—ALOYSIUS BERTRAND, *Gas-
pard de la Nuit.*

LORD, what unto Thy servants shall be given,
    That have so long, in pain and doubt and strife,
For Thee with hand and heart and song hard striven,
    What time Thou givest out the crowns of life?

What time the lances of the light are driven
    Athwart the gloom that holds Life's holiest throne,
What time the curtains of the mist are riven,
    What time the trumpets of the dawn are blown?

We, who to tunes of love and light, unknowing,
  Have chastened all the jarring chords of life,—
We, who with lips with milk and honey flowing,
  Have fed on galls of bitterness and strife,—

We do not ask of Thee, as this our guerdon,
  To live a shining life among Thy blest;
'Twould be for us but shifting of our burden,
  Not the fulfilment of the longed-for rest.

We have no kin with those uplifted faces,
  Those ordered minstrels that before Thee bow,
Set rank on rank upon the holy places,
  With stiff sharp laurel fringing every brow.

For us, no balms of Heaven could stay our yearning,
  No crown of woven lilies and pale palms,
No City with eternal glory burning,
  Set in the golden stress of ceaseless psalms.

Our souls are weary with the stress of seeing,
    Wasted with burning thoughts that throb and
      throng,
Worn with the straining ecstasy of Being,
    That passes through our heart-strings into song.

Our lives are sick with seeing all things' sadness,
    Sad earth beneath us, and sad heaven above ;
Life's sweets to us are but as herbs of madness,
    Sweet poison of the bitter bliss of Love.

Our souls are weary of the changing courses,
    The sick alternative of smiles and tears,
Are weary of the unrelenting forces,
    Are weary of the burden of the years ;

The burden of the winds in river-sedges,
    The burden of the torrents and the sea,
The burden of the woodbirds in the hedges :
    'Time is, Time was, and Time will cease to be !'

Is it as nothing that the same flame courses
  Athwart Thy veins that riots in our own?
Is it as nothing that the selfsame sources
  Of light and life to us as Thee are known?

Shall we 'scape smiting with the 'scape of breath?
  Shall we aye rest from bitter song's fierce smarts?
Will not the song-stress thrill the brain of death?
  Will not the song-pulse throb in our cold hearts?

Lord God, wilt Thou not help us, that have striven
  To do Thy work so hardly and so long?
Wilt Thou not give us rest from Thy high heaven,
  And peace from bitter weaving of sweet song?

Save us, O Lord, before the fire consume us,
  Ere the hot chrism shrivel body and soul!
Let the soft arms of some sweet death entomb us,
  And hold us fast from love and joy and dole!

SUNDOWN.

I

I know not whence it was, nor how it came,
  That I should dream again the sad old dream,
That the recurrent years should bear the same
  Sun-brightened bubbles to my life's dull stream.
So sad and sweet it was, both life and death
  Did mingle in the perfume of its flowers ;
It was compounded of the spring's sweet breath,
  And of the gusty winter's snow-white hours.
The tender cadence of the soft May-wind
  Fanned lovingly the misty winter air ;
The old enchanted Mährchen-blooms combined
  With chill frost-flowers to make it sad and fair.

Armida's garden was it for my feet,

    Its air with magical delights was rife :

'Twas death to me, and yet so living sweet,

    I welcomed death that was more fair than life.

II

' Surely, the bitterness of death is past ! '

    I said, when once that weary dream was o'er ;

' Surely, the corpse of memory at last

    Will rest in peace, and trouble me no more ! '

And so I buried sadly my dead love,

    Laid it to sleep beneath the sands of Time.

It was no phœnix, but a wounded dove,

    (I thought) and would live only in my rhyme.

Alas ! God's essence could not lightly die !

    Its life was quickened by no mortal breath—

It rose again, and filled my life's gray sky

    With all the cold wan loveliness of death.

This phantom is it, whose persistence mars

    The tender beauty of the summer hours,

Whose image blots from me the kindling stars,

    And saddens all the splendour of the flowers.

The months slid swiftly down the year's decline,

    The flowers went drooping to their autumn tomb,

The dying leaves did, dolphin-like, outshine

    With gold and red the summer's lavish bloom.

Springtide and summer had my grief o'erlain

    With primrose-blooms and rose-embalsamed air ;

With dying summer seemed to die my pain,

    And for awhile the cruel foe did spare.

But all too soon I found the ancient fire

    Slept only 'neath the rose and jasmine blooms :

It needed but a breath of dead desire

    To stir old memories in their flowery tombs.

For one light flower-touch of thy white white hand,

    One glance from out thy blue blue eye again,

Could call the dead spring from the shadow-land

    And bid relive for me the vanished pain.

IV

Ay me, Madonna ! we too have our hearts,

    (Strange, seems it not ?) and lose them sometimes, too !

Ay, and they break too, spite of all our arts!
   ' 'Tis true, 'tis pity!   Pity 'tis, 'tis true!'
If I should say in earnest what in jest
   So oft I've told you in an idle song,
Would you not treat it lightly as the rest,
   And deem it fancy?   Yet you would be wrong;
For it is true, my sweet, as God is true,
   I have no heart, no soul, that is not thine!
For it is true, as that the heavens are blue,
   My heart's blood throbbed within the passionate
      line!
If stars give light, my love is star and moon;
If June bear roses, love is my heart's June!

V

If life be sleep, and love the balm of death,
   And faith and beauty be but hour-long dreams;
If hoping faint, as faints the night-flowers' breath,
   And die away upon the years' cold streams;

If dreams be ghast with long-dead hopes and fears,
  And pale sad phantasms dim the glass of time ;
If the unceasing rivulet of the years
  Run no more lucent with the gold of rhyme ;
If all spring-blooms be chalices of woe,
  And all June-sweets with winter's breath be rife,
Ice-flowers shall mock for me the summer's glow ;
  If Love be Death, then Death shall be my life :
Sweet Death, sweet enemy, welcome to my breast,
For, pressing thee, I see, beyond thee, rest.

VI

It is the old complaint we rhymers bear—
  Half-known in heaven, wholly strange to earth—
The banquets of the Immortals now to share,
  And now to wake unto our mortal dearth.
Our souls a twofold burden must sustain ;
  And so, although we have no twofold joy,
Our double life is marred with double pain,
  Our brightest hopes are dulled with earth's alloy.

We must have both—both love and fame—and strive
  The golden chariot of the god of Day
Along the star-emblazoned track to drive,
  With one immortal steed and one of clay.
Poor Phaëtons! no wonder that we fail,
Who would alike in earth and heaven prevail!

VII

O tender beauty of the fleeting years,
  O gilding glory of the sweet sad Past,
God's most effectual healing, that endears
  To us our bitterest memories at last!
O exquisite strange magic, by whose powers
  We live in an immortal wonderland,
Framed in the mist-screen of the fading hours,
  A golden image in a mould of sand!
The memory of past loving gilds our lives;
  New flower-times blossom from the brief annoy;
The olden beauty through a mist revives,
  A faint sweet image of the ancient joy.
The fitful sunheat of the youthful sky
Mellows to sweetness as the years go by.

VIII

I would not have that love of ours revive

(If I could backward tread the years again),

Much as I prized it : life could scarce survive

A second access of the old sweet pain.

I would not, if I could ; and in this strife

I cannot ; for our man's heart has but room

For one short life : and Love itself is life,

And can have but one summer and one bloom.

Is it so short, this love and life of ours ?

Short in its sweetness, in its sadness long ;

And yet we find, among its fleeting hours,

Some that are perfect as a linnet's song.

Dear, it was brief, and left the sweeter peace :

The thought of true love lives, though loving cease.

TO MY SISTER ANNIE.

THE BALLAD OF MAY MARGARET.

OH, sweet is the Spring in coppice and wold,
　　And the bonny fresh flowers are springing !
May Margaret walks in the merry greenwood,
　　To hear the blithe birds singing.

May Margaret walks in the heart of the treen,
　　Under the green boughs straying ;
And she hath seen the king of the elves
　　Under the lindens playing.

‘ Oh, wed thou with me, May Margaret,
　　All in the merry green Maytime,
And thou shalt dance all the moonlit night
　　And sleep on flowers in the daytime ! ’

'O king of the elves, it may not be,

For the sake of the folk that love me;

I may not be queen of the elfland green,

For the fear of the heaven above me.'

' Oh, an' thou wilt be the elfland's queen,

Thy robe shall be blue and golden;

And thou shalt drink of the red red wine,

In blue-bell chalices holden.'

'O king of the elves, it may not be.

My father at home would miss me;

An' if I were queen of the elfland green,

My mother would never kiss me.'

' Oh, an' thou wilt be the elfland's queen,

Thy shoon shall be seagreen sendal;

Thy thread shall be silk as white as milk,

And snow-white silver thy spindle.'

He hath led her by the lilywhite hand
    Into the hillside palace ;
And he hath given her wine to drink
    Out of the blue-bell chalice.

Now seven long years are over and gone,
    Since the thorn began to blossom ;
And she hath brought the elf-king a son,
    And beareth it on her bosom.

'A boon, a boon, my husband the king,
    For the sake of my babe I cry thee !'
'Now ask what thou wilt, May Margaret ;
    There's nothing I may deny thee.'

'Oh, let me go home for a night and a day
    To show my mother her daughter,
And fetch a priest to my bonny wee babe,
    To sprinkle the holy water !

' Oh, let me go home for a night and a day
        To the little town by the river !
    And we will turn to the merry greenwood,
        And dwell with the elves for ever.'

    Oh, out of the elfland are they gone,
        Mother and babe together,
    And they are come in the blithe springtime
        To the land of the blowing heather.

' Oh, where is my mother I used to kiss,
        And my father that oft caressed me?
    They both lie cold in the churchyard mould ;
        And I have no whither to rest me.

' Oh, where is the dove that I used to love,
        And the lover that used to love me ?
    The one is dead, the other is fled ;
        But the heaven is left above me.

' I pray thee, sir priest, to christen my babe
  With bell and candle and psalter ;
And I will give up this bonny gold cup,
  To stand on the holy altar.'

'O queen of the elves, it may not be !
  The elf must suffer damnation,
Unless thou wilt bring thy costliest thing,
  As guerdon for its salvation.'

' Oh, surely my life is my costliest thing !
  I give it and never rue it.
An' if thou wilt save my innocent babe,
  The blood of my heart ensue it !'

The priest hath made the sign of the cross,
  The white-robed choristers sing ;
But the babe is dead ere blessing be said—
  May Margaret's costliest thing.

Oh, drearly and loud she shrieked, as if
    Her soul from her breast would sever !
And she hath gone to the merry greenwood,
    To dwell with the elves for ever.

To my Friend Stephane Mallarmé.

SHADOW-SOUL.

'Destiné à n'avoir que le songe de mon existence, pour moi je ne prétends pas vivre, mais seulement regarder la vie. . . . . Des jours pleins de tris-tesse, l'habitude rêveuse d'une âme comprimée, les longs ennuis qui perpétuent le sentiment du néant de la vie.'—De Senancourt.

'On m'a demandé, "Pourquoi pleurez-vous?" Et quand je l'ai dit, nul n'a pleuré, parce que l'on ne me comprenoit point. . . . . Je soupire parce que la vie n'est pas venue jusqu'à moi.'—Lamennais.

I

There is a tale of days of old

Of how a man, by sorcery,

Wrought to defeat the spells that hold

The soul in bonds, and spirit-free,

At will to wander, naked-souled,

About the earth and air and sea.

Long thus he went (the legend says)
  Until at length some counter-spell,
Flung out upon the worldly ways
  From some abysmal crack of hell,
Seized on him, and, for all his days,
  Doomed him to walk invisible;

Doomed him to pass among the things
  Of life, its joy and strife and dole,
Note all men's hopes and wearyings,
  Feel all their tides beside him roll—
Yet have in all no communings,
  But walk a lone, unfriended soul.

.   .   .   .   .   .

So oftentimes to me it seems
  As if some sad enchantment laid
Upon my life its hand that teems
  With many-mingling spells of shade,
And closed me in a web of dreams,
  Shut out and sole from human aid.

For life has nought to do with me ;
    I stand and watch its pageant pass,
Stream by with pomp and blazonry
    Of many goodly things.   Alas !
Before my gaze its glories flee,
    Like moon-motes on a dream-lake's glass.

Life's guerdons melt beneath my hands ;
    Its sweets fade from me like a mist :
I see folk conquer in the lands ;
    I know men crowned for what I miss'd ;
I see my barren gray life-sands
    Yield to them gold and amethyst.

My life is such a shadow-thing—
    So all unmixed with other lives,
And all men's joy and suffering,
    And all the aims for which life strives—
I think sometimes each hour must bring
    The nothingness whence it derives.

For men pass by me through the air,
   Hot with bright stress of eager aims,
Or furrowed with a sordid care,
   Seeking sweet ease or blazoned names;
Glance at me with a passing stare,
   And vanish from me like swift flames.

My soul is like a wandering light
   Born of marsh-solitudes, and lost,
A hollow flame of heatless white,
   Among a ruddy lifewarm host
Of living fires,—that may unite
   With none, a solitary ghost.

My voice is like the voice of woods,
   When the wind shrills between the pines ;
An echo of sad Autumn moods,
   Wherein the listening ear divines
A tale of endless solitudes,
   Pale vistas stretched in shadowy lines.

My eyes are like some lake of dun,
    Laid in the shadow of the hills ;
Where all around, by day, the sun
    Shines nor may pass athwart its sills
Of firs, but when the day is done,
    The white moon all the silence fills.

II

I gaze around me as I go,
    A pale leaf drifting down the stream ;
Men's lives flit by me in the flow,
    Made dark or bright with shade or gleam :
For me, I feel them not, nor know ;
    Life passes by me like a dream.

I wander with sad yearning eyes
    And heart a-longing for the lost,
(Known but in some dream-Paradise) :
    And ever as my way is cross'd
By folk, my sad soul shrinks and flies,
    Among live men a sighing ghost.

My feet love well to haunt the meads
   And wander where the thrush is loud ;
And yet some sad enchantment leads
   Me aye among the busy crowd ;
And with bent head my life proceeds,
   Where the smoke hovers like a cloud.

And as I wander, once-a-while
   I turn to gaze on folk gone by,
That seem to me not wholly vile,
   Having some kindred in their eye:
They pass me mutely, and I smile ;
   And my heart pulses like to die.

My heart feeds on its own desire :
   The flowers that blossom in my breast
Blow out to pale life, and expire,
   Unknown, unloved, and uncaress'd ;
And the pale phantom-haunted fire
   Burns inward aye of my unrest.

I see twinned lovers, hand in hand,
  Walk in the shadow of the trees ;
Across the gold floor of the sand
  Life passes by with melodies :
Alone upon the brink I stand,
  And hear the murmur of the seas.

I see afar full many a maid
  Walk, musing of the love to come ;
But as I near them, in the shade
  Of my sad eyes they read my doom
Of lonely life, and fly afraid,
  And leave me silent in my gloom.

None may take hold upon my soul :
  No spirit flies from men to me ;
Billows of dreams between us roll,
  Waves spreading out to a great sea :
Neither in gladness nor in dole
  Can our desires conjoinèd be.

I have no heart in their delight ;

   My aim has nothing of their aim ;

And yet the same flowers soothe our sight ;

   The air that rounds us is the same ;

The same moon haunts our ways by night ;

   The same sun rises like a flame.

But over me a spell is cast,

   A charm of flowers and fate and fire ;

My hands stretch out to wastes more vast,

   My dreams through deeper deeps aspire :

Life throbs around me, like a blast

   That sweeps the courses of a lyre.

The merest unregarded thing,

   Dropped into this my solitude,

Fills all my soul with echoing

   Of dreams, as in some haunted wood

A pebble's plash into a spring

   Is by the circling air renewed

III

And yet there stirs a great desire
   For human aid within my breast;
Men's doings haunt me like a fire,
   My heart throbs loud with their unrest;
And now and then, as hope draws nigher,
   My soul leaps to them, unrepress'd.

For though my feet in silence move
   Alone across this waste of hours,
My heart strains hopeward like a dove,
   My soul bursts out in passion-flowers;
My life brims o'er with a great love,
   Alone in this wide world of ours.

My full soul quivers with a tide
   Of songs; my head heaves with a hum
Of golden words, that shall divide
   The dusk, and bid the full light come.
Alas! men pass me, careless-eyed;
   And still my lips are pale and dumb.

I go beneath the moon at night,
　. Across the grey deserted streets;
My heart yearns out in the pale light,
　A new hope pulses in its beats;
Meseems that in the radiance white
　My soul a like pale spirit meets:

As if the trance of the sad star
　Were the mute passion of some spright,
That (like my own) some Fate did bar
　From all Life's fruits of dear delight;
Some soul that aye must mourn afar,
　And never with its love unite.

And then my heart flowers out in hope:
　A new sweet music sweeps along
The courses of my soul; the scope
　Of heaven is opened to a throng
Of long-pent thoughts; and all my hope
　Pours forth into a flood of song.

K.

Sometimes, too, as I walk alone,

   The mists roll up before my eyes,

And unto me strange lights are shown,

   And many a dream of sapphire skies ;

The world and all its cares are gone :

   I walk awhile in Paradise.

But in the day unfolded clear,

   When the fresh life is all begun,

My soul into the old sad sphere

   Falls off; my dull feet seem to shun

Once more the daylight, and I fear

   To face the frankness of the sun.

Alone and dumb, my heart yearns sore ;

   I am nigh worn with waste desire :

I stand upon a rocky shore,

   Watch life and love sail nigh and nigher ;

Then all pass by for evermore,

   And leave me by my last hope's pyre:

IV

And yet I grieve not nor complain ;
   The time for me has long gone by,
When I could half assuage my pain
   By giving it delivery :
My grief within my breast has lain
   Unspoken, and my eyes are dry.

I am confirmed in this my fate ;
   I lock my love within my breast,
Nor look to find my soul a mate,
   Nor match with hope my hope unblest :
I am content to watch and wait,
   Impassible in my unrest.

Long have I ceased the idle stress
   Towards the rending of my gloom :
I am made whole in loneliness ;
   I lay no blame on this my doom ;
I curse not, if I do not bless :
   My life is silent as the tomb.

And yet (methinks) some day of days,
   The silence that doth wrap me round,
May at its heart of soundless ways
   With some faint echoing resound
Of my own heart-cry, and the rays
   Of a like light in it be found.

Haply, one day these songs of mine
   Some world-worn mortal may console
With savour of the bitter wine
   Of tears crushed out from a man's dole ;
And he may say, tears in his eyne,
   There was great love in this man's soul !

Ay, bitter crushed-out wine of love,
   Pressed out upon his every word,
A note as of some sad-voiced dove,
   As of some white unfriended bird,
Dwelling alone in some dim grove,
   Whose song no man hath ever heard :

But only the pale trackless sea
  And the clear trances of the moon
Have quivered to his melody;
  And for the rapture of the tune,
Their attributes, sad sanctity
  And peace, they gave to him for boon;

So that his sadness, in the womb
  Of the mild piteous years, has grown
A holy thing; and from the tomb,
  Where in the shade he lies alone,
(As was in life his lonely doom)
  The seed of his desire has blown

Into a flower above his grave,
  Full of most fair and holy scent;
Most powerful and sweet to save
  And to heal men from dreariment.

And I shall turn me in my grave,
  And fall to sleep again, content.

A BIRTHDAY SONG.

I

WHAT shall I say to my dearest dear,

On the sweetest day of the whole sweet year?

   Shall I tell her how dainty she is, and sweet,

   From her golden head to her silver feet?

Love of my loves, shall I say to her—

   Till the breeze catch tune and the birds repeat

The chime of my song—thou art bright and rare,

 (Eyes of the gray and amber hair)

   Who is so white as my love, my sweet?

     Who is so sweet and fair?

II

Ah, no ! for my song would faint and die,

Faint with a moan and a happy sigh,

   For a kiss of her lips so clear and red,

   For a touch of her dainty gold-wrought head,

      And a look of her tender eye !

And even the words, if words there were said,

Would fail for the sound of her lovely name,

Till the very birds should flout them to shame,

   That they strove to render silver with lead,

      To image with snow the flame !

III

So e'en I must sing her over again

The old old song with its one refrain,

   The song that in Spring like the cooing dove

   Has nothing for burden but just ' I love.'

Go, my songs, like a silver rain,

   And flutter her golden head above,—

Sing in ner walks and her happy day,

Fill all her dreams with the roundelay,

   ' I love ' and ' I love her,' again and again,

      ' I love her,' sorry or gay !

IV

Is she thinking of me, my lady of love?
(Heart of my heart, is the day enough
    For the thought and the wish of her daintiness
    And the memory of the last caress?)
Do her lips seek mine, my gold-plumaged dove—
My little lady with glass-gray eyne—
    In long sweet dreams of the night to press
From the grapes of delight Love's golden wine?
    Does thought seem more and the world seem less,
        While her hand strays, seeking mine?

V

Fly to her, fly, O my little song!
(Fly to her quickly; the way is long,
    And your little dove-coloured wings are weak)
    Whisper the things that I cannot speak,
Say what I would, if *my* wings were strong
    And the heaven were near to seek:
Take all the tender fancies that lie
And flower in my heart so silently;
    Sing her the love I can never speak
        Wholly, but in a sigh!

THE BALLAD OF SHAMEFUL DEATH.

' Le regard calme et haut,
Qui damne tout un peuple autour d'un échafaud.'

BAUDELAIRE.

I

I GO to an evil death, to lie in a shameful grave,

And I know there is never a hope, and never a God
that can save ;

Yet I smile, for I know that the end of my toil and my
striving is come,—

I shall sleep in the bosom of death, where the voice
of the scorners is dumb.

II

I go in the felons' cart, with my hands bound fast
     with the cord,
And nothing of brave or bright in the death that I ride
     toward :
The people clamour and jeer with a fierce and an evil
     glee,
And the mothers and maids that pass do shudder to
     look on me.

III

For the deed that I did for men, the life that I
     crown with death,
Was a crime in the sight of all, a flame of the pest-
     wind's breath ;—
And the good and the gentle pass with a sad and a
     drooping head,
As I go to my punished crime, to lie with the felon
     dead.

IV

But lo! I am joyful and proud, as one that is newly
crowned :

I heed not the gibes and the sneers and the hates that
compass me round ;

I come not, with drooping head, to the death that a
felon dies—

I come as a king to the feast, with a deathless light in
mine eyes !

V

I ride with a dream in my eyes and the sound of a
dream in mine ears,

And my spirit wanders again in the lapse of the bygone
years ;

I smile with the bygone hope, and I weep for the bygone grief,

And I weave me the olden plans for the world's and
the folk's relief.

VI

I build me over again the time of my yearning
    youth,

When my heart was sick for men's grief, and my glad-
    ness failed me for ruth ;

For I saw that their lives were weary and maddened
    with bitter toil,

And there came no helper to heal, no prophet to purge
    the soil.

VII

I mind me how all the joys, a man in his manhood's
    prime

May have in the new sweet world and the strength of
    his blossom-time,

Were saddened and turned to gall by the cry of the
    world's lament,

That withered the roses' bloom, and poisoned the
    violets' scent.

VIII

My heart is full of the thoughts that gathered within
    my soul,
And the anguish that held my life at the sight of my
    fellows' dole;—
I mind me how, day by day, the passion grew in my
    breast,
The voices cried in my sleep, and gave my spirit no
    rest.

IX

·It rises before me now, in its fragrance ever the
    same,
The day when my soul found peace, and my yearning
    soared like a flame,
The day when my shapeless thought took spirit and
    speech and form,
The day when I swore alone to front the fire and the
    storm.

X

It rises before me now, the little lane by the wood,

With the golden-harvested fields, where the corn in its

    armies stood,

The berries brown in the hedge, the eddying leaves in

    the breeze,

And the spirits that seemed to speak in the wind that

    sighed through the trees.

XI

The path where I went alone, in the midst of the

    swaying sheaves,

Through the landscape glowing with gold and crimson

    of Autumn leaves ;

The place where my full resolve rose out of my tears

    and sighs,

Where my life was builded for me, and my way lay

    clear in my eyes.

XII

I mind me the words I spoke, the deeds that I did
   to save,

The life that I lived to rescue the world from its living
   grave ;

I mind me the blows I smote at the thronèd falsehood
   and blame,

The comfort I spoke for the lost, the love that I gave
   to shame.

XIII

I mind me of all the hates that gathered about my
   strife,

The gibes that poisoned my speech, the lies that
   blackened my life,

The fears that maddened the folk, the folly that shrank
   with dread

From the love I spoke for the live, the hope I spoke
   for the dead.

XIV

For the men, with their purblind souls, chose rather
to live and die .

In the olden anguishful slough, to groan and weary
and sigh

In the old familiar toil and the old unvarying hate,

Than rise to a joy unknown, a love to free them from
Fate.

XV

And the words that I spoke for love, the deeds that
I did for hope,

The future I showed for life in the new sweet cre-
dence's scope,

They deemed them a tempting of hell, a blasphemy
and a crime,—

They thought the angel a fiend, that called them out
of their slime.

XVI

The yearning that cried in their breasts, that met my
own like a flood,

They thought to quench it with fire, to stay its passion
with blood,

To deaden my voice with death, (their own should be
silent then,)

And so I come to atone for the love that I bore to
men.

XVII

My enemies laugh in their joy, as the people jeer at
my fate;

They know not the seed of love that lies at the heart
of hate:

They give me hatred for love, and death for the life I
brought;

But I smile, for I know that love shall come at the
last, unsought.

XVIII

I look far on in the years, and see the blood that I
    shed

Crying a cry in men's ears, crying the cry of the dead;

I see my thought and my hope fulfilling my work for
    men

In the folk that jeer at me now, the lips that spat at
    me then.

XIX

I know that for many a year my life shall be veiled
    with shame,

That many an age shall hate me, and make a mock of
    my name ;

I know that the fathers shall teach their children many
    a year

To hold my hope for a dread and know my creed for
    a fear.

XX

But I know that my work shall grow in the darkness
  ever the same ;
Its seed shall stir in the earth in the shade of my evil
  fame ;
My thought shall conquer and live, when the sound of
  my doom is fled,
And my name and my crime are buried, to lie with
  the unknown dead.

XXI

Wherefore I smile as I go, and the joy at my heart is
  strong,
And I gaze with a peace and a hope on the cruel glee
  of the throng ;
I live in my thought and my love, I conquer time with
  my faith,
And I ride with a deathless hope to crown my living
  with death.

XXII

I loved thee, beautiful Death, in the fresh sweet time
of the spring,
And I will not fail from my troth in the wind of the
axe's swing ;
I come to thy bridal bed, O Death my beloved, I
come !
I shall sleep in thine arms at the last, when the voice
of the scoffers is dumb.

XXIII

O friends that are faithful yet ! if your love shall
bear me in mind,
With a graven stone on the tomb where I sleep with
my felon kind,
Write me as one that fell in the way of a punished
crime,
' Hated of men he died, in the heart of the evil time !'

XXIV

And yet I will not be thought to glose o'er my full
stern fate,

Or leave weak words of complaint for the ages that
lie in wait.

Rase out the final words ; I will stand by the first
alone—

'Hated of men' shall stand for my monument on the
stone !

XXV

I was never in love with the praise, nor afraid of the
censure of fools,

Mean they as well as they may, they were ever the
dastard's tools.

Strike out the words of complaint ; I will stand by the
rest alone—

'Hated of men' shall be for the roll of my virtues on
stone !

XXVI

And yonder on in the years, some few of the wise,
    peradventure,

Shall read in the things laid bare the truth of my life-
    long venture,

Shall see my life like a star in the shrouding mists of
    the ages,

And set my name for a light and a patriot's name in
    their pages.

XXVII

And then shall the clearer thought and the tenderer
    sight fulfil

The things that I left unsaid, the words that are lack-
    ing still:

A poet shall set my name in the gold of his noble
    rhyme—

' Hated of men he died, in the heart of the evil time ! '

IN THE NIGHT-WATCHES.

'The days are prolonged, and every vision faileth.'—EZEKIEL.

I

I CRIED to myself in the night,
  'O God ! is the day at hand ?
My spirit longs for the light,
  I weep in the shadow-land ;
For the black night brings to me bitter tears,
The shadows call up the vanished years,
The past troops by on its many biers,
  Ghosts in a dismal band.

II

Very sad is the day,
    I said ; but the night I weep—
Weep for the woes that slay,
    The terrors that compass sleep :
For the sounds of the wailing never cease,
The tides of the tears for aye increase,
The shadows will never have rest and peace,
    What though the grave be deep.

III

I lay me down in the dusk,
    After the day is done,
And the clouds in their hodden husk
    Have folded the golden sun :
Now shall I cease from travail, I say,
Now shall I put off the woes of day,
Now shall I bury me far away,
    Under the shadows dun.

IV

Vulture-winged cometh the dark,
  Brimming the air with the night;
And I, I lie and I hark,
  And strain my eyes for a sight.
I watch and hope, with a faith unfed,
I lie and dream of a life unsped,
I live in the things that are long since dead,
  I fancy the darkness light.

V

I strive with a mighty stress
  To hold the terror from me,
To ward off the ghastliness
  Of night and its mystery;
I spread out my hope like a sail on seas
That toss in the void to an unknown breeze,
I strain my faith for a hope that flees
  And a joy that may not be.

VI

But pitiless cometh the gloom
  And the gray-winged spectres of Death,
And stealthily creepeth the doom,
  And the worm that remembereth :
The night grows full of the shapes of ill,
Strange phantoms moan at the window-sill,
The voices wail at the wild wind's will ;
  My heart grows chill with their breath.

VII

The moon is a ghostly face,
  The wraith of a radiance dead,
That wanders across the space,
  Dead, but unhouselèd :
The stars are the eyes of the sad still sprights,
The lone lost souls that wander anights,
And mock the day with their weirdly lights
  And their flitting drearihead.

VIII

There wavers about my bed,
 In the lurid gloom of the night,
The awful host of the dead,
 Prisoned in spectral white :
I read in their eyes the dreadful scrolls,
The record of all the wrong that rolls,
And the pain that gathers about the souls,
 The terror that darkens light.

IX

I read in their sightless eyes
 The record of burning tears,
The writing that never dies,
 The graven anguish and fears :
I hear in their silent mouths the sound
Of the wails that are mute and the cries that are
  drowned
In the sombre heart of the passionless ground
 And the dead unburied years.

X

One by one, without end,
 On through the night they go :
As each through the gloom doth rend,
 I see a face that I know ;
I feel a sorrow a man has known,
A brother-pain that has burnt and grown,
Through the long sad years and the midnights
  lone,
 To a spectral shape of woe.

XI

I see the life of my fear,
 A ghastly wraith of the dead ;
I hear his cry in my ear,
 Though never a word be said.
I feel a pang that was dumb before,
I stand and gaze from a shadow shore,
And I hear the waves of the death-sea roar,
 And I know my heart has bled.

XII

The terrors revive again,
　　The victims moan on the blast :
I weep with the world in pain,
　　I bleed with the wounded past ;
My heart is heavy with memories,
My breast is weary with hopeless sighs ;
The moon weeps tears of blood in the skies,
　　And the stars with grief are ghast.

XIII

My heart leaps up to my mouth
　　With a mighty suffering ;
My soul is sick with a drouth,
　　A nameless horrible thing :
I may not seize on the shape of my fear,
I may not close with my visions drear
And lay my wraiths on the saving bier ;—
　　Ah, that my lips could sing !

XIV

Ah, that my soul could soar
  On the living pinions of song,
And open the prison door
  Of life for that ghastly throng!
Ah, would I could call each shape by his name,
That my voice could chase them with singing flame
To the quiet graves from whence they came
  And the slumber cold and long!

.   .   .   .   .

XV

The stress of the things of life
  With a throbbing agony stirred;
The night and its spectral strife
  Took spirit and speech and word:
'Shall none be potent to save?' it cried;
'Shall no light dawn in the darkness wide?
Shall no voice roll back the shadow-tide?
  No saving song be heard?

XVI

'Lo!' and it said, 'For the stress,
   The love fades out in men's hearts,
And there fadeth the loveliness
   From singers' and limners' arts ;
For a man must work for the bitter bread,
Till his life has forgotten its goodlihead,
Till his soul is heavy with doubt and dread,
   And the bloom of his dream departs !

XVII

'Surely a singer shall weep,
   And a poet shall weave his verse
With a pity tender and deep,
   With love instead of a curse ;
For all things thirst for a word of ruth,
The sweet spring even has lost its youth,
The world is very dreary in truth,
   And pain grows daily worse.

XVIII

' Lo ! if a prophet should come,

And a singer to speak for men,

To give a voice to the dumb,

The world should be shriven then !

The folk should be freed from the unknown woes,

The griefs that are crimes, and the pain that grows

To a fruit of hate from the unshared throes,

And the unassoilzied pain !

XIX

' The tyrant should recognise

His spirit's bitterness,

The sound of the agonies

That crush his heart with their stress,

The pain that has gathered to rage in his breast,

In the stifled sobs of the folk opprest ;

The slayer should know his hopes unblest

In his victim's hopelessness.

XX

'The folk should turn in a day
    To love and its years of gold :
The tyrant should cease to slay,
    The years of anguish be told ;
For the eyes of the folk should be cleared to know
That crime and sin and tyranny grow
From a common root in a common woe,
    A sorrow dumb and cold.

XXI

' Alas for the folk unsung !
    In the dark and sorrowful ways !
The earth is weary and wrung
    For lack of the poet's lays !
O hearts of men, has the world no tears,
Is there none to weep for the vanished years,
And the waste life troubled with doubts and fears,
    And the weary dying days ? '

M

XXII

Alas ! for I may not speak !
    Alas ! for my lips are dumb,
And the words that the spell would break,
    Alas ! for they will not come !
I lie and groan with a dumb desire,
I toss and burn with a sleepless fire,
And I long for the sound of a golden lyre
    And a poet's voice to come !

XXIII

I long for a poet's voice
    To lighten the sunless ways,
To say to the earth, ' Rejoice !'
    To hearten the dreary days,
To burst the chains of the silentness
That holds the world in its dismal stress,
To rend from being the prides that press,
    And the terrors that amaze !

XXIV

I wait and am waiting still,

  I lie and suffer and long;

How long shall the silence fill

  The haunts of sorrow and wrong?

How long shall the great dumb host of the sad

Hold sternly aloof, whilst the heaped years add

To their anguish, for want of a singer had

  And a succour? O God! how long?

A MONOTONE.

I

A LARK in the mesh of the tangled vine,
A bee that drowns in the flower-cup's wine,
A fly in the sunshine,—such is man.
All things must end, as all began.

II

A little pain, a little pleasure,
A little heaping-up of treasure,
Then no more gazing upon the sun.
All things must end that have begun.

III

Where is the time for hope or doubt?
A puff of the wind, and life is out.
A turn of the wheel, and rest is won.
All things must end that have begun.

IV

Golden morning and purple night,
Life that fails with the failing light.
Death is the only deathless one.
All things must end that have begun.

V

Ending waits on the brief beginning.
Is the prize worth the stress of winning?
E'en in the dawning the day is done.
All things must end that have begun.

VI

Weary waiting and weary striving,
Glad outsetting and sad arriving;
What is it worth when the goal is won?
All things must end that have begun.

VII

Speedily fad es the morning glitter;
Love grows irksome and wine grows bitter.
Two are parted from what was one.
All things must end that have begun.

VIII

Toil and pain and the evening rest,

Joy is weary and sleep is best ;

Fair and softly the day is done.

All things must end that have begun.

PANTOUM.

(Song in the Malay manner.)

THE wind brings up the hawthorn's breath,
   The sweet airs ripple up the lake :
My soul, my soul is sick to death,
   My heart, my heart is like to break.

The sweet airs ripple up the lake,
   I hear the thin woods' fluttering :
My heart, my heart is like to break ;
   What part have I, alas ! in spring ?

I hear the thin woods' fluttering ;
  The brake is brimmed with linnet-song :
What part have I, alas ! in spring ?
  For me, heart's winter is lifelong.

The brake is brimmed with linnet-song ;
  Clear carols flutter through the trees ;
For me, heart's winter is lifelong ;
  I cast my sighs on every breeze.

Clear carols flutter through the trees ;
  The new year hovers like a dove :
I cast my sighs on every breeze ;
  Spring is no spring, forlorn of love.

The new year hovers like a dove
  Above the breast of the green earth :
Spring is no spring, forlorn of love ;
  Alike to me are death and birth.

Above the breast of the green earth,

   The soft sky flutters like a flower :

Alike to me are death and birth ;

   I dig Love's grave in every hour.

The soft sky flutters like a flower

   Along the glory of the hills :

I dig Love's grave in every hour ;

   I hear Love's dirge in all the rills.

Along the glory of the hills

   Flowers slope into a rim of gold :

I hear Love's dirge in all the rills ;

   Sad singings haunt me as of old.

Flowers slope into a rim of gold

   Along the marges of the sky :

Sad singings haunt me as of old ;

   Shall Love come back to me to die ?

Along the marges of the sky
   The birds wing homeward from the East :
Shall Love come back to me to die ?
   Shall Hope relive, once having ceas' d?

The birds wing homeward from the East;
   I smell spice-breaths upon the air :
Shall Hope relive, once having ceas'd ?
   It would lie black on my despair.

I smell spice-breaths upon the air ;
   The golden Orient-savours pass :
Hope would lie black o1 my despair,
   Like a moon-shadow on the grass.

The golden Orient-savours pass ;
   The full spring throbs in all the shade :
'Like a moon-shadow on the grass,
   My hope into the dusk would fade.

The full spring throbs in all the shade ;
   We shall have roses soon, I trow ;
My hope into the dusk would fade ;
   Bring lilies on Love's grave to strow.

We shall have roses soon, I trow ;
   Soon will the rich red poppies burn :
Bring lilies on Love's grave to strow ;
   My hope is fled beyond return.

Soon will the rich red poppies burn ;
   Soon will blue iris star the stream :
My hope is fled beyond return ;
   Have my eyes tears for my waste dream ?

Soon will blue iris star the stream ;
   Summer will turn the air to wine :
Have my eyes tears for my waste dream ?
   Can songs come from these lips of mine ?

Summer will turn the air to wine,
  So full and sweet the mid-spring flowers !
Can songs come from these lips of mine ?
  My thoughts are gray as winter-hours.

So full and weet the mid-spring flowers !
  'The wind brings up the hawthorn's breath.
My thoughts are gray as winter-hours ;
  My soul, my soul is sick to death.

A SONG OF DEAD LOVE.

I

THERE came to me a dream in the midnight
  Of a fair shape beseen with glittering hair,
  The semblance of a woman, very fair,
Yea, and most sorrowful; for all the light
Within her eyes was faded for despite

II

  Of worldly woe, and all her bloom was fled,
For grieving over ghosts of dead delight,
And wearying for Love and all his might,
  That in the petals of the rose lay dead,
  Mourned over by the lily's heavy head.

III

' If any love,' to me the shape did say,
    (And as she spoke I turned me in my bed,
    Wondering to look upon her goodlihead)
' Most meet it is, I should upon thee lay
  The task of warning him from love away.

IV

' For bitter sooth it is that Love doth lie
All sadly buried from the eyes of day,
Under the shredded petals of the May
  And with his death did ease of lovers die,
  And nought is left for them but tear and sigh.

V

' Wherefore, if one have the desire of it,
    Knowing not the doom that in the thing doth lie,
    This strait commandment unto thee give I,
  That thou with song do of Love's death let wit
  Those foolish souls that still their lives do knit

VI

' About an idle woman's gold red hair,
And in the empty courts of Love do sit,
Watching the torches for his funeral lit,
  That they should win their senses to forbear
  From loving aught, because the thing is fair.

VII

' For, of a truth, henceforth the end of love
  Shall be no more as it of old hath been,
  Since healing Love is dead, that aye did wean
Sore hearts to solace. Whoso tastes thereof,
He shall be hungered all his days for love,

VIII

' And shall in nowise come to ease his pain ;
For since Love's light is faded from above
The world into the grave, his silver dove—
  That wont whilom all lovers to assain
  With balm, and quickly make them whole again,

IX

' Nestling soft wings against their wounded hearts—
　　Has for the sorrow of its Lord's death ta'en
　　The semblance of a falcon, all a-stain
　With blood and milk, that with fell rancour darts
　His ruddy beak into each heart that smarts

X

' With lover's woe ; and delving in the breast,
Doth tear and lacerate the inward parts,
Until all hope of future ease departs
　　From the sad soul, and men are all opprest
　　With unsalved love unto the utterest.

XI

' Wherefore, sing thou and warn the folk of ill !
　　And I : ' O lady, would my tongue were blest
　　With happy words ! But lo! I have no rest
　For agonies of love, that all doth fill
　My sleepless soul, and all its cruel will

XII

'Doth wreak on me, to bring me to despair.

How shall I ward from men the darts that kill,

When I myself am of their poison still

    Nigh stricken unto death? O lady fair!

Teach me how I may win the bird to spare,

XIII

" And then I will make shift for men to sing

    As thou dost bid !' But she, with such an air

    Of pity, answered, ' First the song must fare,—

And haply salve shall rest upon its wing.'

Wherefore I made this song, awakening.

THE KING'S SLEEP.

I

'Bury me deep,' said the king,
 ' Deep in the mountain's womb ;
   For I am weary of strife.
  Hollow me out a tomb,
      So that the golden sun
       Pierce not the blackness dun,
         Where I shall lie and sleep ;
 Lest haply the light should bring
   Again the stirring of life,
  Or ever the time is come
        To waken.   Bury me deep.

II

' Let not the silver moon
   Search out the graven stone
      That lieth above my head
   In the tomb where I sleep alone.
         Nor any ray of a star
         Come in the night to unbar
            The gates of my prison-sleep.
I shall awake too soon
      From the quiet sleep of the dead,
   When the trumps of the Lord are blown.
         If you love me, bury me deep.

III

' I feel in my heart of hearts
      There cometh a time for me,
         Deep in the future's gloom,
      When there no more may be

Rest for my weary head,
When over my stony bed
The wind of the Lord shall sweep.
And scatter the tomb in parts ;
And the voice of the angel of doom
Shall thrill through and waken me
Out of my stirless sleep.

IV

' For a king that has been a king,
That has loved the people he swayed,
Has bound not his brows in vain
With the gold and the jewelled braid ;
Has held not in his right hand
The symbol that rules the land,
The sceptre of God for nought !'
He may not escape the thing
He compassed : in death again
His sleep is troubled and weighed
By wraiths of the deeds he wrought.

V

' And if he has evil done,

There may he lie and rest

Under the storied stone,

Slumber, uneasy, opprest

By the ghosts of his evil deeds,

Till Death with his pallid steeds

Have smitten the world with doom :

And the moon and the stars and the sun

Will leave him to sleep alone,

Fearing to shine on him, lest

The wicked arise from the tomb !

VI

' But if the ruler be wise,

Have wrought for his people's good

Sadly and like a god ;

Whenever the plague-mists brood

Over the kingless land,

When fire and famine and brand

Are loose, and the people weep,

They cry to the king to rise;

And, under the down-pressed sod,

He hears their pitiful cries,

And stirs in his dreamful sleep.

VII

'And the sun and the stars and the moon

Look down through the creviced tomb,

And rend with their arrows of light

The sepulchre's friendly gloom,

Stirring the life again

In pulse and muscle and vein;

And the winds that murmur and sweep

Over his resting-place, croon

And wail in his ear: "The night

Is past, and the day is come;

O king, arise from thy sleep!"

VIII

' And the sleeper murmurs and sighs,—

Rest is so short and sweet,

Life is so long and sad,—

And he throws off his winding-sheet :

The gates of the tomb unclose,

And out in the world he goes,

Weary and careful, to reap

The harvest ; in hero-wise

To garner the good, and the bad

To burn, ere the Ruler shall mete

Him yet a portion of sleep.

IX

Great is the Master of Life,

And I bow my head to His will !

When He needs me, the Lord shall call,

And I shall arise and fill

The span of duty once. more !
But now I am weary and sore
With travail and need of sleep ;
And I fear lest the clangour and strife
Upon me again should fall,
Ere sleep shall have healed my ill.
I pray you, bury me deep !'

X

So the good king was dead,
And the people wrought him a grave
Deep in the mountain's womb,
In a place where the night-winds rave
And the centuries come and go,
Unheard of the dead below ;
Where never a ray might creep—
In the rocks where the rubies red
And the diamonds grow in the gloom,
They hollowed the king a tomb,
Low and vaulted and deep.

XI

And there they brought him to lie :
  With sobbing and many a tear,
    The people bore to the place
    The good king's corpse on the bier.
      They perfumed his funeral glooms
      With lily and amaranth blooms,
        In a silence sweet and deep ;
They piled up the rocks on high,
      And there, with a smile on his face,
With doubt and sadness and fear,
        They left the monarch to sleep.

XII

Onward the centuries rolled,
  And the king slept safely and sound
    In the heart of the faithful earth,
    In the still death-slumbers bound :

And the sun and the moon and the stars
Looked wistfully down on the bars
Of the sepulchre quiet and deep,
Where he lay, while the world grew old,
And death succeeded to birth,
And heard not an earthly sound,
And saw not a sight in his sleep.

XIII

And it came to pass that the Wind
Spake once, and said to the Sun :
'O giver of summer-life !
Is not the time nigh run,
And the measure of God fulfilled,
Wherein He, the Lord, hath willed
The king should arise from sleep ?
I go in the night and I find
The folk are weary of strife,
And joyless is everyone,
And many a heart doth weep !'

XIV

But the Sun said, shaking his hair,

His glorious tresses of gold :

' Brother, the grave is deep ;

And the rocks so closely do fold

The king, that we may not win

A place where to enter in

And trouble his slumber deep ! '

And the Wind said : ' Where I fare,

The rays of the sun can creep,

Through the thin worm-holes in the mould,

And rouse the king from his sleep ! '

XV

Then the Moon and the Stars and the Sun

Arose and shone on the grave,

And it was as the Wind had said :

Yea, up from the vaulted cave

The worms had crept in the night,
　And opened a way for the light
　　And the winds of the air to creep.
And they entered, one by one,—
　Yea, down to the house of the dead,
Through cranny and rock they clave,
　　To wake the king from his sleep.

XVI

And the king turned round in his dream,
　As he felt the terrible rays
　　Creeping down through the mould
In the maze of the false worms' ways ;
　　And he quaked as the light drew near,
　And he called to the earth for fear,
　　To aid him his rest to keep ;
For the time he had slept did seem
　But an hour, nor the wheels of gold
Had circled the span of days
　　When he should arise from sleep.

·XVII

But the mother all-faithful heard
　　The dreaming call of the king,
　　　　And she seized on the wandering rays,
　　And of each one she made a thing
　　　　Of jewelries, such as grow
　　　　In the dim earth-caves below,
　　　　　　From the light kept long and deep;
For she loved the man, and she feared
　　The fateful glitter and blaze
Of the light too early should bring
　　　　The dead from his goodly sleep.

XVIII

She moulded pearls of the moon
　　And diamonds of the sun;
　　　　Rubies and sapphires she made
Of the star-rays, every one.

Yea, there was none might 'scape
Some luminous jewel-shape
Of all the rays that did creep
Down through the earth, too soon
To rend the sepulchre's shade ;
But she seized on them all, and none
Might trouble the dead man's sleep.

XIX

Then did she weave him a crown
Of silver and cymophane,
And in it the gems she set
For a sign that never again,
Till God should beckon to him,
On the silence quiet and dim
Of the sepulchre low and deep,
Should the rays of the stars look down
To trouble his rest.   And yet
The centuries come and wane ;
And the king is still in his sleep.

CADENCES.

(MINOR.

I

THE ancient memories buried lie,
  And the olden fancies pass ;
The old sweet flower-thoughts wither and fly,
And die as the April cowslips die,
  That scatter the bloomy grass.

II

All dead, my dear !   And the flowers are dead,
  And the happy blossoming spring ;
The winter comes with its iron tread,
The fields with the dying sun are red,
  And the birds have ceased to sing.

III

I trace the steps on the wasted strand

Of the vanished springtime's feet :

Withered and dead is our Fairyland,

For Love and Death go hand in hand—

Go hand in hand, my sweet !

CADENCES

II

(MAJOR.)

I

Oh, what shall be the burden of our rhyme,

And what shall be our ditty when the blossom's on
the lime?

Our lips have fed on winter and on weariness too
long:

We will hail the royal summer with a golden-footed
song!

II

O lady of my summer and my spring,

We shall hear the blackbird whistle and the brown
sweet throstle sing,

o

And the low clear noise of waters running softly by
    our feet,
When the sights and sounds of summer in the green
    clear fields are sweet.

III

We shall see the roses blowing in the green,
·The pink-lipped roses kissing in the golden summer-
    sheen ;
We shall see the fields flower thick with stars and
    bells of summer gold,
And the poppies burn out red and sweet across the
    corn-crowned wold.

IV

The time shall be for pleasure, not for pain ;
There shall come no ghost of grieving for the past
    betwixt us twain ;
But in the time of roses our lives shall grow together,
And our love be as the love of gods in the blue
    Olympic weather.

A BALLAD OF THE STARS IN MAY.

I

THE streamlet rushes,
The May-bloom blushes,
The moonlight silvers the lea ;
The stars are bright
In the sweet spring-night :
I only lie sadly, a dreaming wight,
Alone with my pain
In the silver rain
That falls from the hawthorn-tree.

II

The starflowers seem,

With their sapphire gleam,

To beckon and nod to me :

Their runes I fashion

To the tune of my passion,

And question their lamps, as they float above,

'Shall I see her ever again, my love?

Will she ever come back to me?'

III

The stars gleam bright

In the purple night,

They twinkle with mocking glee :

Their keen rays dart

To my bleeding heart

And stir it again.to the olden smart,

As they write their answer in light above,

'Thou'lt see her never again, thy love!

She'll never come back to thee!'

IV

The moonlight glitters,

The streamlet twitters,

The night-blossoms sway and sing :

The spring-night gladness

But mocks my sadness,

The earth is drunk with celestial madness,

And the flowers are singing the old old song

Hour after hour through the whole night long,

With the olden eery ring.

V

The flowers are singing,

The elf-bells ringing

Over the blossomy lea :

' False stars, ye have heard

That mocking word

From the mouth of some faithless gossiping bird ;

For ye sing me again

The same old strain

She sang long ago to me ! '

VI

The stars gaze down

On the meadows brown,

They twinkle with baleful glee ;

I read in their runes

Still the same old tunes ;

They answer ever,

‘ Thou'lt see her never,

She'll never come back to thee ! ’

VII

The streamlet rushes,

The May-bloom blushes,

With ecstasy pants the air ;

The land is bright

In the sweet spring-night ;

I only lie sadly, a dreaming wight,

Whilst the stars look down

Through the tree-shade brown,

With the olden mocking stare.

AREOPAGITICA.

'Parle aux oppresseurs ; enveloppe-les des plaintes, des gémissements, des cris de leurs victimes ; qu'ils les entendent dans leur sommeil et les entendent encore dans leur veille ; qu'ils les voient errer autour d'eux comme de pâles fantômes, comme des ombres livides ; que partout les suive l'effrayante vision ; que ni le jour ni la nuit elle ne s'éloigne d'eux ; qu'à l'heure du crépuscule, lorsqu'ils s'en vont à leurs fêtes impies, ils sentent sur leur chair l'attouchement de ces spectres et qu'ils frissonnent d'horreur.'

LAMENNAIS, *Une voix de prison.*

I

I WENT in the night of the summer, under the woods
    in the gloaming,
  Under the crown of the oaks, and the solemn shade
    of the pines ;
And I watched the lamps of the angels over the firma-
    ment roaming,
  And read the secrets of fate in their inscrutable
    signs.

II

And lo! as I went in the shade, at the hour when the
    sky is darkened
  And the silver disc of the moon under the cloudline
    dips,
I heard a sound in the air, as if the forest-world heark-
    ened;   ·
  A power was born in my breast, and a spirit spoke
    from my lips,

III

Saying, 'Come forth and be judged, O ye that have
    darkened living!
  Ye that have stolen the joy and the sweetness from
    pleasant life!
I tell you, the hour is at hand that shuts you out from
    forgiving,
  When you shall answer for all you've sown of an-
    guish and strife!

IV

'Stand forth, kings, in your purple ! stand forth, priests,
　　in your shame !

　Merchants and slavers, and all that thrive on the
　　blood of your kind !

All that have helped in men's bosoms to stifle the
　　sacred flame,

　Have stolen men's fruit of gladness and left but the
　　bitter rind !

V

' Stand forth and hear the wrongs, as the bards and
　　sages have told them,

　Your fellows have done to men, in the dusk of the
　　bygone time !

Listen ! and tremble for fear, as the eyes of your soul
　　behold them

　Bound in the singing hell of the poet's terrible
　　rhyme ! [1]

---

[1] ' Kein Gott, kein Heiland erlöst ihn je
　　Aus diesen singenden Flammen ! '—HEINE.

VI

'Stand forth, kings, in your purple; lords of nations
    and armies!
  Ye that have held in your hands the keys of evil
    and good!
Ye that have ransacked life to search and see where
    the charm is,
  Have rifled the blossoms of hell to stay your hun-
    ger with food!

VII

'Ye that have not been content with lust and riot and
    madness,
  Have sucked for a sharper delight in your people's
    anguish and fears,
Have made your life joyous with pain, and glad from
    your servants' sadness,
  Fair with the horror of blood, sweet with the bitter
    of tears!

VIII

'Lo! I will summon you up from the heart of the
glooms infernal!
Up from your darksome graves, up from your slumbers of stone!
I wi'l make your shame for a sign and your anguish a
thing eternal!
I will spare no whit to your souls of all the ills ye
have sown!

IX

'Stand forth and be judged, ye merchants! that heap
up gold without measure!
That wither to sparkling dross the golden fruit of
the years!
That gather the incense of sighs and the sweat of blood
for your treasure,
That mould into gold our troubles, and make coined
gold of our tears!

X

'Ye that have thrived on the pain and the grinding
need of the toilers,

Have bounden life with your burdens, that hold it
tearless and dumb !

Ye that, to lengthen the scope and the harvest-time for
the spoilers,

Have shut the portals of Life, lest Death the de-
liverer come !

XI

'Stand forth and be judged, ye priests ! that suck the
life of the nations !

That darken the azure of heaven into the gloom of
a pall !

That fetter men's health and their strength with your
prayers and your imprecations,

That poison their hope with doubting, and mingle
their gladness with gall !

XII

‘ Ye that have ever been ready to do the will of the
  tyrants,
 To toll, at a monarch's bidding, fair Freedom's
  funeral knell !
Ye that to strangle thought and to shackle its upward
  aspirance,
 Have lengthened the struggles of life into the
  horrors of hell !

XIII

‘ Lo ! I will summon up the pale sad shapes without
  number,
 That fell and died without speaking beneath your
  pitiless hands !
I will call up the unnamed victims that load the earth
  with their cumber,
 That fill the fields with their anguish and shade
  with their sorrow the lands !

XIV

' Ye think ye have silenced them now ; and the heart
within you rejoices !

Ye think that justice is dead, and none shall rebuke
you again !

I tell you, I hear in my ears the dumb inarticulate
voices

Speak with clearness of thunder from ocean and
forest and plain !

XV

' I tell you, the hollow graves, where the tyrants that
went before you

Lie in the prison-sleep of the middle sepulchre's
gloom,

Are bound with the selfsame fate that threatens and
hovers o'er you,

Ring with the coming curse and quake with the
coming doom !

XVI

'For the doom that their victims wrought not, the
 curse that they died unspeaking,
 Grew and shall grow for aye with their mouldering
  forms in the earth :
The vengeance they could not wreak, the winds and
 the worms are wreaking,
 Breaking the sleep of the dead with a fierce and
  terrible mirth !

XVII

'But lo ! a more horrible doom and a nearer vengeance
 are waiting
 For you, if ye turn not away from your sins and
  humble your heads !
For the fate, that is ripe for you, shall wait no death
 for its sating,
 Shall grow in your living hearts, and lie in your
  silken beds !

XVIII

' I tell you, the soul of the dead and the wailing dumb
  in their dying
  Is gathered again by the winds and garnered up in
  the flowers !
I tell you, their yearning is hid, and their curses and
  prayers are lying,
  Ready to burst on your heads, in the womb of the
  coming hours !

XIX

' For a season shall be when the meat that ye eat shall
  be sad with their curses,
  The drink that ye drink shall be deadly and bitter
  to death with their tears,
The garments ye wear shall burn and eat to your
  hearts like Dirce's,
  The sights that ye see shall be as a fire that mad-
  dens and sears !

XX

' The eyes of the dead shall look, with a doom and
 an accusation,

From the eyes of the friends you love, and the
 maidens that kiss your lips !

The voice of the dead in your ears shall clamour
 without cessation ;

The shade of their hate shall darken your lives with
 its fell eclipse !

XXI

' And if you shall say : *The grave will give us the peace
 we burn for,*

*Will bring us the senseless sleep and the rest un-
 troubled by thought ;*

*We will sleep with our fathers of old, and have the ease
 that we yearn for,*

*Free from the memory's pain and the wraiths of the
 things we wrought ;*

XXII

' The doom that you laid on others shall fall on your-
　　selves, unsparing !
　　The anguish ye felt of old shall seem as nought to
　　　　the new !
For the earth, that shall wrap you round, shall shut
　　　　you in from all sharing,
　　Shall hold you fast in her arms, where nothing can
　　　　succour you !

XXIII

' The lapses ye had in life, when the anguish failed for
　　a second,
　　And the memory slid away from the moment's
　　　　glitter and glow,—
Ye shall never have them again, when once the
　　　　angel hath beckoned,
　　When once your bodies are dust and your heads in
　　　　the tomb are low !

XXIV

' For the wraiths of the wrongs you wrought shall compass you round, unceasing ;
The spirits of all the dead you crushed in your
bitter strife
Shall fold your souls in a fire and an anguish for aye
increasing,
Shall fashion for you in death a new and terrible
life !

XXV

' Wherefore I bid you repent. For the time draws nigh
to the reaping ;
The harvest ripens apace, and the sickle lies in the
tares.
I bid you turn from your sins with fear and sorrow
and weeping,
Whilst yet the trumpets are dumb, and the fire of
the judgment spares ! '

SIR ERWIN'S QUESTING.

I

'OH, whither, whither ridest thou, Sir Erwin?
The glitter of the dawn is in the sky,
And I hear the laverock singing
Where the silken corn is springing
And the green-and-gold of summer's on the rye.'

II

' O lady fair, I ride towards the setting;
For the glamour of the West is on my heart,
And I hear a dream-voice calling
To the land where dews are falling,
And the blossoms of the springtime ne'er depart.'

III

'Oh what, oh what thing seekest thou, Sir Erwin ?

Is life no longer pleasant to thy soul ?

Am I no more heart's dearest,

Though the summer skies are clearest

And the gold of June is fresh on copse and knoll ? '

IV

' O sweet, I seek the land where love is holy

And the bloom of youth is ever on the flowers ;

The land where joy is painless

And the eyes' delight is stainless,

And the break of love faints never in the weary

noontide hours !'

V

' Oh rest awhile, oh rest awhile, Sir Erwin !

The hills are yet ungilded by the sun.

Oh tarry till the morning

Have pierced the mists of dawning

And the weariness of noon be past and done !'

VI

'O lady fair, I may not tarry longer !
  The sun is climbing fast above the grey,
      And I hear the trumpets blowing
      Where the eastern clouds are glowing
  And the mists of night are breaking from the city
      of the day !'

VII

Far out into the greenwood rides Sir Erwin,
  Oh, far into the wild wood rideth he !
      And there meet him sisters seven,
      When the sun is high in heaven,
  And the gold of noon is bright on flower and tree.

VIII

Oh, wonder-lovely maidens were the seven !
  With mantles of the crimson and the green ;
      With red-gold rings and girdles,
      And sea-blue shoes and kirtles,
  And eyes that shone like cornflowers in their locks'
      corn-golden sheen.

IX

'Oh, light thee down and dwell with us, heart's dearest!

And we will sing thee wonder-lovely songs!

And we will strew with roses

The place where thy repose is,

And teach thee all the rapture that to our love

belongs!

X

'Oh, light thee down and dwell with us, heart's dearest'

We have full many a secret of delight:

Thy day shall be one sweetness

Of love in its completeness,

And the nightingale shall sing to thee the whole

enchanted night!'

XI

'Oh, woe is me! I may not stay, fair maidens;

My quest is for a country far and wild;

The land where springs the Iris,[1]

Where the end of all desire is,

And the thought of love lives ever undefiled.'

[1] There is a legend that the more distant-seeming end of the rainbow begins in Fairyland.

XII

'Oh, light thee down and dwell with us, heart's dearest!
Thou wilt wear thy youth to eld in such a quest :
For it lies beyond the setting,
In the land of the Forgetting,
In the bosom of the everlasting rest ! '

XIII

Far on into the greenwood rides Sir Erwin,
Oh, far into the wild wood rideth he !
And he sees a fair wife sitting
At the hour when light is flitting,
And the gold of sunset gathers on the sea.

XIV

Oh, very fair and stately was her seeming,
And very sweet and dreamful were her eyes !
And, as she sat a-weaving,
She sang a song of grieving,
Full low and sweet to anguish, mixt with sighs.

XV

'Oh, tell me what thou weavest there, fair lady,

I prithee tell me quickly what thou art!'

'I am more fair than seeming,

And I weave the webs of dreaming

For the solace of the world-awearied heart.'

XVI

'Oh, prithee tell me, tell to me, fair lady,

What song is that thou singest, and so sweet?'

'I sing the songs of sorrow

That is golden in the morrow,

And I charm with them the sad hours' leaden feet.

XVII

'Oh, light thee down and dwell with me, heart's dearest!

Thou hast wandered till thy face is furrowed deep;

But I will charm earth's cumbers

From the rose-leaves of thy slumbers,

And will fold thee in the lotus-leaves of sleep.'

XVIII

'Oh, woe is me ! oh, woe is me, fair lady !
  A hand of magic draws me on my quest
      Towards the land of story,
      Where glows the sunset-glory,
  And the light of love fades never from the West.'

XIX

'Oh, light thee down and stay with me, heart's dearest !
  Thine eyes will lose their lustre on the way ;
      For it lies far out to yonder,
      Where the setting sun dips under,
  And the funeral pyres are burning for the day.'

XX

Oh, far thorough the greenwood rides Sir Erwin,
  Oh, far out of the wild wood rideth he !
      And he comes where waves are plashing,
      And the wild white crests are dashing
  On the pebbles of a gray and stormy sea.

XXI

Far down towards the tide-flow rides Sir Erwin,
  Oh, far adown the shingle rideth he !
      And he sees a shallop rocking
      Upon the wild waves' flocking,
  And an ancient steersman sitting in the lee.

XXII

Oh, very weird and gruesome was that steersman,
  With hair that mocked for white the driven snow !
      The light of some strange madness
      Was in his eyes' gray sadness,
  And he seemed like some pale ghost of long ago.

XXIII

'Oh, sail with me ! oh, sail with me, Sir Erwin !
  Thou hast wandered in thy questing far enough.
      I will bring thee where Love's ease is
      For ever, though the breezes
  Blow rudely, and the broad green way be rough.'

XXIV

' Reach hand to me, reach hand to me, old steersman !
  I will sail with thee for questing o'er the main.
    Although thine eyes look coldly,
    I will dare the venture boldly ;
  For I weary for an ending of my pain.'

XXV

Oh, long they rode on billows, in the glory
  Of the gold and crimson standards of the West !
    So came they, in the setting,
    To the land of the Forgetting,
  Where the weary and the woful are at rest.

XXVI

' Oh, what can be this land that is so peaceful,
  That lies beyond the setting of the sun ?
    I hear a dream-bell ringing,
    And I hear a strange sweet singing,
  And the tender gold of twilight's on the dun.

XXVII

'Oh, what are these fair forms that float towards me?
  And what are these that clasp me by the hand,
      As if they long had sought me?
      And what art thou hast brought me
  O'er the ocean to this dream-enchanted strand?'

XXVIII

'Fair knight, this is the land of the Hereafter;
  And the name that men do know me by is Death:
      For the love, from life that's flying,
      Lives ever with the dying,
  And the stains of it are purged by 'scape of breath!'

A BACCHIC OF SPRING.

'Le beau Dionysos, dont le regard essuie
Les cieux et fait tomber la bienfaisante pluie,
Qui s'élance, flot d'or, dans les pores ouverts
De notre terre et fait gonfler les bourgeons verts.'
                    THÉODORE DE BANVILLE.

I

OUT of the fields the snowdrops peep :

'To work, O land !

Awake, O earth, from the white snow-sleep,

Shake off the coverlet soft and deep ;

Spring is at hand !

Thou hast slumbered the months away long enough ;

'Tis time for the winter rude and rough

To die and give way

To the bloomy May :

Awake and shake off the tyrant gruff ! '

Up from the numbing clasp of the snow !
　　Shake off the winter weather !
The breath of the year grows warm apace,
As the snowflakes melt from his fresh young face,
　　And the eastern moorlands are all aglow
　　　　With their budding heather !
Already the swallows are calling, ' Cheep ! cheep !
All things are waking from their long sleep,
　　　　We and the spring together !'

See where the battle-host of the blooms
　　　　Waits for the fray !
See where the cowardly tyrant glooms !
He knows the scent of those soft bright dooms,
　　　　That say to him, ' Hence away ! '
Over the meadows their squadrons glitter,
　　Orange and purple and white and blue,
　　Jewel-helmed with the diamond-dew,
　　　A fairy army of sweet spring roses,
　　　Of bluebell-blossoms and pale primroses,

Spreads out its ranks in the balmy air,

Whilst the lark and linnet and blackbird twitter

A quaint war-march for each fairy Ritter,

That troops in the alleys fair!

II

Wearyful winter is gone at last,

With its wild winds sighing,

And the blooms of the spring are creeping fast :

Primrose and cowslip and windflower-bells

Broider the grass in the cool wood-dells ;

Cloud-roses over the sky are flying.

Evoë ! the chill of the year is dying !

Good-bye to the bitter blast !

Iö ! the hillocks are mad with bliss,

As the new sweet stirring

Quickens their hearts with the vernal kiss !

Silver and azure and golden green

The meadows shine in the warm spring-sheen,

And the music of myriad wings is whirring,

As the birds, that fled from the winter frore,

Back to the isle with the silver shore

Hasten from spice-forests far away

In the Indian seas,

To revel in blossom-embroidered May,

As the flower-hosts chase out the winter gray

From the newly wakened leas!

Bacchus returns from the eastern skies!

(Welcome his train with their bright wood-sheen)

Evoë! he brings us the golden prize,

The charm of the Indian queen

He battled so long for and won at last!

He brings us the spell that unchains the flowers

And loosens the wheels of the golden hours

When the power of the frost is waning fast,

When the chill snowflakes from the landscape fly,

And the dying eastwinds wearily sigh,

'Alas! our winter is past.'

Q

See ! to the eastward his lance-points beam !

Iö ! the time is near !

Evoë ! the winter wanes like a dream,

As the diamond helms of the Bassarids gleam,

And the May-blooms glow in the sun's full stream,

That glitters on every spear !

Already I hear their voices' hum,

And the pipe and clang of their silver reeds,

And their songs of the spring-god's sweet flower-deeds,

As back from the golden East he leads

His sea-shell car with the tiger steeds !

Evoë ! the spring is come !

Evoë, Lyæus ! the spring is here !

Onwards they come apace !

See how the landscape, bare and sere,

Flushes at once with a golden bliss,

As the earliest touch of the warm spring kiss

Gilds with a tender grace

The grand old winter-enwounded trees,

That throb and sway in the balmy breeze,

Sweet from the flower-strewn plains,

As the radiant train of the wine-god sweeps

Through the inmost heart of the woodland deeps,

And the 'wildering thrill of the springtide creeps

Up through their frost-dried veins !

A SOUL'S ANTIPHON.

I

My soul burst forth in singing,
  My heart flowered like a rose ;
Chimes of sweet songs fled ringing
  Along the forest close.
Is it the new year springing?
  Is it the May that blows?
  No ; it was none of those.

Among the trees came flying
  A spirit like a flame ;
A sound of songs and sighing,
  Mixed, round his presence came—
A sound of sweet airs dying,
  The music of a name,
  Fainting for its sweet shame.

A white shape wreathed with flowers,
　A winged shape like a dove;
Hands soft as peach-bloom showers;
　Eyes like an orange-grove
In whose enchanted bowers
　The magic fire-flies rove:
I knew his name;—'twas Love.

'O soul!' I said, 'the voices
　That flutter in thy breast,
The yearning that rejoices
　In its own vague unrest,
Are all in vain: the choice is
　'Twixt Life and Love's behest.
　Choose now, which is the best.'

The winged white Love came calling,
　With words as sweet as lays
When hawthorn-snows are falling
　About the forest ways.

His speech was so enthralling,
  Such spells were in his gaze,
  My heart flowered with his praise.

He came to me with kisses,
  And looked into my eyes;
My soul brimmed up with blisses,
  But with the bliss came sighs,
As when a serpent hisses
  Beneath flower-tapestries
  And moss piled cushion-wise.

The sad old thoughts came flocking
  Up to that look of his :
For memory and its mocking,
  I could not smile, I wis;
It was like the unlocking
  Of doors on an abyss
  Wherein old living is.

It was like grief recounting
   The happy times of yore ;
It was like gray waves mounting
   A lost sun-golden shore,
Like sad thoughts over-counting
   The sweet things gone before,
   The days that are no more.

And as I looked with sighing
   Into the sweet shape's eyes, ·
I saw a serpent lying
   'Mid balms of Paradise ;
I knew my dole undying,
   The presage sad and wise,
   The worm that never dies.

Love laughed and fled, a-leaping,
   Between the flower-flushed breres,
And left my sad thoughts keeping
   The vigil of the years :

My soul burst out in weeping ;
  I saw my hopes and fears .
  Troop by, enbalmed in tears.

II

My soul burst forth in weeping,
  My heart swelled like a sea ;
There came sad wind-notes sweeping
  Across the golden lea :
Is autumn past, and reaping?
  Is winter come for me ?
  No, no, it cannot be.

Among the trees came slowly
  A spirit like a flower,
A lily pale and holy,
  White as a winter hour :
Sad peace possessed him wholly;
  Around him, like a sower,
  He cast a silver shower ;

A shower of silver lilies,
  Each one a haunting thought :
It was as when a rill is
  Across waste rose-bowers brought,
And all the heart's grief still is,
  And one has pain in nought :
  Such peace their perfumes wrought.

'O soul !' I said, 'the sadness
  That is in this one's breath
Is sweeter than the madness
  That round Love fluttereth :
This one shall bring heart's gladness
  And balms of peace and faith ;
  For lo ! his name is Death.'

The pale sweet shape came strewing
  Flower-tokens on the grass ;
His face was the renewing
  Of love in a dream-glass ;

His speech was like bird-wooing,
    When moonlight-shadows pass.
    My soul sighed out, ' Alas ! '

He came to me with sighing,
    My hand in his he took ;
My soul wept nigh to dying,
    For all his piteous look :
Yet in his eyes was lying
    Peace, as of some still brook
    Laid through a forest-nook.

The memories of past sorrow
    Brimmed up my eyes with tears ;
I could not choose but borrow
    Fresh grief from the waste years :
And yet some sweet to-morrow
    Smiled through, as when rain clears
    Off, and the sun appears.

It was as if one, peering
   Into a well of woe,
Saw all the shadow clearing
   From the brown deeps below—
Saw sapphire skies appearing,
   And woods with moss aglow,
   And spring in act to blow.

With tearful looks, I, gazing
   Into the sad shape's eyes,
Saw a new magic tracing
   New lovely mysteries;
I saw new hope upraising
   A new love's Paradise,
   And clear moon-silvern skies.

My soul fled forth in singing,
   My heart flowered like a rose;
Death smiled, with sweet tears springing,
   'Twixt smile and smile that rose.

His arms closed round me, clinging :

Peace came, and clipt me close—

Peace, such as no love knows.

SAILORS.

Across the deep-blue sea
We go a-voyaging,
With silver wake a-lee
The world environing;
From Sonda's island-sea,
From India's skies of gold,
Unto the Arctic cold.

The little stars denote,
With fingers all of gold,
Which way our keel shall float,
Which way our sails unfold.
With canvas wings unrolled,
Like birds as white as snow,
Across the waves we go.

Our thoughts fly to the shore
We're leaving far away,
The youthful loves of yore,
Our mother's locks of gray;
But the light ripple's play,   ·
With its soft murmurous sweep,
Soon lulls our grief asleep.

The husbandman doth plow
A niggard soil and sealed;
The vessel with its prow
Divides our azure field,
And the rich sea-deeps yield
Withouten toil or woe
Coral and pearls eno'.

A wondrous life ours is !
Cradled in this our nest,
We traverse the abyss,
On the sea's boundless breast.

Skimming the billows' crest,

Across the great blue waste,

Alone with God we haste.

From Théophile Gautier.

THE BALLAD OF THE COMMON FOLK.

1

KINGS, in your turn that will be judged some day,
  Think upon those that lack of all delight ;
Have pity on the folk that love and pray,
  That know no joy, that weary day and night,
  That delve the soil, that die for you in fight.
Their life is like the damnèd souls' in fire,
That never know the taste of their desire.
  The luckiest barefoot and an hungred go ;
The scorching sun, the rain, the frost, the mire—
  For poor folk all is misery and woe.

II

Like beasts that wear their lives in toil away,
, Within his hovel is the wretched wight.
Will he for once make merry and be gay,
    For harvest reaped or for a bridal night,
    Thinking at least to mark one day with white,
Down swoops his lord upon the luckless sire,
With outstretched hand and greed that yet more dire
    From satisfaction of its lust doth grow,
And like a vulture empties barn and byre.
    For poor folk all is misery and woe.

III

Have pity on the wretched fool whose play
    Unknits your brow, the fisher that for fright
Starts, when the levin leaps athwart his way,
    The dreamy blue-eyed maiden, humbly dight,
    That spins before her door in the sunlight : .
Have pity on the mother's void desire,

R

Clasping her starving infant nigh and nigher,

   (Ah God ! that little children should die so !)

To warm its frozen limbs for lack of fire.

   For poor folk all is misery and woe.

ENVOI.

For all poor folk I crave your pity, sire :

The peasant lying in the frozen mire,

   The nun that telling o'er her beads doth go,

And for all those that lack their heart's desire.

   For poor folk all is misery and woe.

From Théodore de Banville.

A SONG OF WILLOW.

I

Love and Life have had their day,

Long ago ;

Hope and Faith have fled away

With the roses and the May ;

This is but an idle show :

Come away !

II

Seekest thou for flowers of June,

Roses red ?

Listenest for the linnet's tune ?

Here the night-fowl wails the moon ;

Here are lilies of the dead,

Tear-bestrewn.

III

Thinkest Love will come again,
　　Fresh and sweet,
With the apple-blossoms' rain?
Many a day dead Love has lain,
　　Folded in the winding-sheet.
　　　　Hope is vain.

IV

See, Death beckons from the gloom,
　　(Come away !)
Life is wasted from its room,
Love is faded from its bloom ;
　　Come and nestle in the gray
　　　　Of the tomb.

V

Come away !　The bed is laid,
　　Soft and deep ;

In the blossomed linden's shade,
Underneath the moon-pale glade,
    In the quiet shalt thou sleep,
        Unaffrayed.

VI

Kiss thy love upon the lips
        Once again.
I will fold thee in the eclipse
    Of the night where shadows stray,
And sleep healeth heart and brain :
        Come away !

THE HOUSE OF SORROW.

THERE is a story, told with many a rhyme
    In dusty tomes of old,
Of how folk sailed, in the fresh ancient time,
    Into the sunset's gold—

Into the land of western hope they sailed,
    To seek the soul of joy,
That from the modern life of men had failed,
    Crushed by the dull annoy

Of pain and toil; the gladness of the age,
    When Love was king on earth,
And summer, midmost in the winter's rage,
    In men's warm hearts had birth :

This did they seek.   Beyond the sun, they thought,
    Deep in the purple West,
There lay the charm of joyance that they sought,
    Awaiting some high quest :

Charm to be won by earnest souls and pure,
    And brought anew to life ;
Wherewith provided, one might hope to cure ·
    Men's endless dole and strife.

So from the chains of love and toil and gold,
    The love of wife and maid,—
All human ties had they cast loose,—unrolled
    The fluttering sails, and weighed

Swift anchor, steering towards the dying day,
    Hope in their hearts most high
That they should win the charm that therein lay
    For men's sake, ere to die

The angel bade them.   And the high heart fell
    Not in them, though the wind
Blew fresh and swift for many a day, the swell
    Ran pearled the keel behind,

Along the emerald, and the golden dawn
    Sank ever sad and pale
Into the westward and was gone,
    Whenas the dew did fail ;

And nothing met their vision, save the streaks
    Of gold and crimson, wound
About the westward, when the dead day's cheeks
    Flushed with the sun, that drowned

His glory sullenly in amber foam ;
    And the dim mists that lay
Along the sapphire marges of the dome
    Of heaven, in the gray

Of the pale dawning ; and the narrowing wheel
    Of sea-birds round the sail,
And silver fish that played about the keel,
    With many a golden scale

And fin of turquoise glancing through the spray :
    But never the fair line
Of green and golden shores, the long array
    Of palaces divine

That held the dream of their long venturings,
    Rose in the changeful West ;
But still the ship sped with its silver wings
    Over the fretted crest

Of the slow ripple ; still the sea was green
    And calm on every side,
And the swift course unto their vision keen
    Brought but the weary wide

Gray circle bounded by the silver foam ;
    And still they looked and hoped
For the fair land where the true joy had home
    Wherefor they sighed and groped

Amid the mirk of living.   Ever pale
    And paler grew the skies,
And less refulgent in its crimson mail
    The hour when the day dies :

And every day the dawn was tenderer
    And sadder in its white
And rosy pudency ; and still the stir
    Of the sad winds of night

Crept closelier on the noontide, till the day
    Was hardly much more glad
Than the pale night ; and morning was as gray
    As when the hours are sad

With stormy twilight.   So at last they came—
    Whenas the purple flame
Of dying daylight slept upon the crest
    Of sea, that in the West

Swept to the sunward, as it were to catch
    The day's last fluttering sigh—
In sight of a fair city, that did match
    The tender amethyst sky,

Pale purple with the setting.   Very fair
    And lucent were the walls;
And in the evening the enchanted hair
    Of some pale star, that falls

From azure heights of mystery, did seem
    To compass it about
And wrap it round with glamours of a dream,
    Golden sad webs of doubt :

So that for those sweet clinging veils of mist,
    Amber and vaporous,
One could but faintly note the amethyst
    And jewels of the house

That rose with many a stately battlement
    Out of the pulsing sea,
And could but dimly trace the forms that went,
    Most fair and sad to see,

About the silver highways and the quays
    Of gold and chrysoprase,
Tender and lovely as the shapes one sees,
    In some sweet autumn haze,

Flit, in the gloaming, through the enchanted air;
    When there is none to know,
Save some pale poet, that may never dare
    To tell the lovely woe,

The tender ecstasy of sad delight
    He has seen pictured there
Upon the canvas of the pale twilight,
    Under the evening air.

But they that sailed in that enchanted ship,
    No whit cast down, drew sail
And came to where the amber-polished lip
    Of the gold shore grew pale

Under the kisses of the purpled sea :
    And there they landed all ;
And wandering inward through the blazonry
    Of portico and hall,

They came to where the soul of sadness sat,
    Throned in a woman's form—
Most holy and most lovely—and forgat
    In her sweet eyes the worm

Of yearning that had gnawed their hearts so long,
And knew at last,
From her low whispers and the sad sea's song,
That thither had Life past

As to its goal-point : for the golden thing
That they had lacked on earth,
Was not (as they had deemed) the god rose-wing
Of gladness and of mirth—

The god of vine-and-ivy trellised brow
And sunny orient eyes—
For he did haunt men ever, did they know
But to be linnet-wise :

But that best gift of the Immortal Ones,
That men have lost for aye ;
The pure sweet sadness that we know but once,
And then we come to die.

The mingled love and pain we Sorrow call,
    There did it dwell alone,
The tender godlike pain once known to all,
    Now but to poets known.

There sit they through the long unwearying years,
    At that fair lady's knees,
Lulled by the ripple of her songs and tears
    And the sweet sighful breeze

Into forgetting of the things of life
    And the weird shapes that fleet
Across its stage of mingled dole and strife ;
    For sorrow is so sweet,

There is no gladness that may equal it,
    Nor any charm of bliss.
And fain would I from the pale seekers wit
    Which way the steering is

That may, with helm and sail and oar pursued,

    Bring me where she doth dwell,

The lovely lady of that solitude.

    Is there no one can tell?

FRANCE.

(JANUARY 1871.)

AH, land of roses ! France, my love of lands !
　　How art thou fallen from thy high estate !
Bleeding, thou writhest in the Vandals' hands,
　　And the crowned spoiler sitteth in thy gate.
　　My heart is sore for thee : I weep and wait ;
Shall not God help thee and deliver thee
From whom the world has taken liberty ?

Thou France, the fairest and the holiest,
　　The knightly people, hating every wrong,
Hast thou so long redeemed the world opprest,
　　Sacring the Right with sword and sword-swift song,
　　Hast thou so many a year for us been strong
To slay the doubt, to unveil the hopeful years,
And now, alas ! sittest alone in tears ?

Alone and bleeding ; for the Wrong prevails,
  The dragon-crested Wrong, that, like a snake
Growing, shall strangle in its loathsome scales
  All loveliness of life, all hopes that break
  The grinding chains of toil, all songs that wake
Under the flower-blue skies, all knightly use,
And level all to its abhorred abuse.

For this is he that in the name of Right
  Has strangled many a nation ; this is he
That holds all noble faith, all honour light,
  That let the lust of his rapacity ;
  He that, exulting from a bloody sea,
Calls God his helper ; he that, void of shame,
Robs, lies, and murders in the Holy Name !

Alas, that men are blind, or will not see !
  Our Saviour France, the lover of mankind,
Lies bound and bleeding, straining piteously
  Against the brutal tyrant : on the wind
  Her cries for help assail us ; but we, blind

With some prophetic blindness, turn aside,
Saying, ' She sinned ; her doom let her abide.'

And yet take heart, O land of many tears !
   We are not powerless that love thee well :
Our songs float up to Heaven, and God hears
   Our psalms of vengeance.   Fair and terrible,
   The hour shall come to break the evil spell :
Live ! for we love thee.   Shall not love be strong?
Arise and conquer, fortified with song !

Our love thy banner !   We are manifold :
   Though men despise us, we are strong in faith,
We that are taintless with the greed of gold,
   We for whom Love is mightier than Death ;
   We hail thee with a hope !   As with one breath,
We bid thee conquer—'spite the scorn of men—
And slay the twy-necked Vulture in his den !

SONGS' END.

I

THE chime of a bell of gold
  That flutters across the air,
The sound of a singing of old,
The end of a tale that is told,
  Of a melody strange and fair,
  Of a joy that has grown despair :

II

For the things that have been for me
  I shall never have them again ;
The skies and the purple sea,
And day like a melody,
  And night like a silver rain
  Of stars on forest and plain.

III

They are shut, the gates of the day ;

   The night has fallen on me :

My life is a lightless way ;

I sing yet, while as I may !

   Some day I shall cease, maybe :

   I shall live on yet, you will see.

This is my House of Dreams—a house of shade,
  Built with the fleeting visions of the Night:
  Here have I set my youth, and all its white
Sad memories—in this dwelling that I made
With idle rhyme, as lonely fancy bade.

  If any wonder at the strange sad might
  The God of Visions holds upon my sight,
And set himself my weak song to upbraid
  For all the wailing notes therein that teem,
I pray him of his favour that to lands
  Of sunnier clime he wend; for things that seem
Are here the things of life, and give commands
To living; for a dream is on my hands,
  And on my life the shadow of a dream.

LONDON : PRINTED BY
SPOTTISWOODE AND CO., NEW-STREET SQUARE
AND PARLIAMENT STREET

By the same Author, fcp. 8vo. cloth, price 3s. 6d.

INTAGLIOS: SONNETS.

By JOHN PAYNE,

AUTHOR OF 'THE MASQUE OF SHADOWS,' AND OTHER POEMS.

'With the exception of Mr. Rossetti, Mr. Payne is almost the best English sonnet writer that we have had since Mrs. Browning published her "Sonnets from the Portuguese." . . . Dante is his model, to whom he dedicates the first sonnet in the volume ; and there is a clear, pleasant echo of the "Vita Nuova" in every one of the seventy-three that follow it. . . . He writes like a poet, mastering the difficulties and satisfying the requirements of the sonnet with great skill. Here and there the antiqueness of his expression looks like affect-ation, but all flaws are atoned for by the exquisite thrills and touches of song he often utters. The fourteen sonnets entitled "Madonna dei Sogni" are, perhaps, the best in the volume, and each of the fourteen helps to work out the thought of the poem as compactly and gracefully as does each of the fourteen lines in each separate sonnet.'—*The Examiner.*

'The confidence we expressed in our review of "The Masque of Shadows and other Poems," that Mr. Payne would ultimately acquire distinction as a poet, remains unshaken. . . . Here, as there, no cultured reader could fail to detect the presence of the spirit of true poetry. . . . There is uniformity of tone throughout the whole. . . . Two or three of his sonnets are perfect in delicacy and lyrical sweetness. . . . We believe that he has a natural voice of rich tones, and this we hope to see him exercise to its fullest extent.'—*The Athenæum.*

'We are grateful to Mr. Payne for rousing us from the somewhat drowsy state into which we had fallen as we perused page after page of poets gifted with that fatal fluency of language which is so convenient a cloak to the want of thought. If he is at times obscure, there is much in his sonnets that is as clear as it is beautiful. They show no signs of hasty work ; on the contrary, they are polished as only a scholar loves to polish. . . . Some of Mr. Payne's lines are wonder-fully musical.'—*The Saturday Review.*

'In "Intaglios" are noticeable the same features which elicited admiration and applause in "The Masque of Shadows." Elevation of thought and literary culture are combined with so delicate and airy a fancy that one is almost inclined to object to the hardness implied in the title, forgetting for the moment that the term is to be applied rather to the execution than to the matériel.'—*The Illustrated London News.*

'There is much that is noteworthy in these sonnets—subtle fancy, scholarly execution, and a quaintness of thought which, although occasionally more curious than beautiful, is not without a charm. Mr. Payne has more grace than strength, more of tenderness and refined feeling than of sustained power. He does not speak to the multitude ; but the careful workmanship displayed in this little volume will excite the admiration of all students of poetry.'—*The Pall Mall Gazette.*

'The sonnet seems to suit the genius of Mr. Payne's poetry. Its narrow limits and the rigidity of its form do something to check the wild luxuriance of his fancy. . . . But the intrinsic faults and beauties of such as he writes are of course not materially affected by any variation of form. . . . A highly poetical style, made positively gorgeous by a word-painting which uses liberally the most brilliant colours, attracts the reader with great promise of beauty. . . . Here is a sonnet which Mrs. Browning might have written. It is called "Jacob and the Angel," and is said to have been suggested by "a design by J. T. Nettleship."'—*The Spectator.*

Fcp. 8vo. cloth, 7s.

THE MASQUE OF SHADOWS,

AND OTHER POEMS.

By JOHN PAYNE.

'This is a book of genuine imagination; the qualities which characterise it are precisely those which distinguish poetry from less elevated forms of composition. Its most marked feature is an exuberance of fancy and invention, controlled by a chastened literary taste. It consists of four poems of considerable length. The first, from which the volume takes its name, exhibits those qualities in the highest degree. . . . The second, "The Rime of Redemption," is more condensed in style and artistic in execution. It is a wild legend in the form of a ballad, narrated with admirable point, and full of spirit and fire. "The Building of the Dream" and "Sir Floris" are somewhat deficient in these respects. They are successions of exquisite pictures, but there is too little action. In style and general effect they are most successful reproductions of the metrical romances of the middle ages. The volume abounds with proofs of culture and scholarship, no less than of poetical power.'—*The Illustrated London News.*

'"The Masque of Shadows" has already won for Mr. Payne no mean place among the poets of the day.'—*The Spectator.*

'Mr. Payne's "Masque of Shadows" is, in spite of its evanescent title, the most durable book of the set of five. Two other poems, "The Building of the Dream" and "Sir Floris," both of considerable length, unite with the "Masque" to make up a volume of uncommon merit. The story of Squire Ebhardt, in "The Building of the Dream," and of Sir Floris's winning his place among the guardians of the San Graal in the mystic city of Sarras, are very striking—and often very beautiful—reproductions of some of the best thought and best work of mediæval Christianity. Mr. Payne's lines abound with words of curious and semi-French archaism; but these are never dragged in; they suit the general effect, and clearly come from the overflow of a memory steeped in the romance literature whence they are drawn. Those who think poetry nothing without the piquancy of what is called, in cant phrase, a "profound human interest," will see nothing in Mr. Payne's book to admire. A less exacting criticism, though in general almost as much oppressed by new books of verse as Sir Floris was by the novel monsters that flapped about him with their buffetings, may take pleasure in admitting that these poems not only deserve to be read, but will bear reading over again: and, if they must be ranked among the voluminous works of minor poets, they merit the worthiest place there.'—*The Saturday Review.*

'Four poems, very different in character and conception, make up this curious and remarkable book, "The Masque of Shadows," "The Rime of Redemption," "The Building of the Dream," and "The Romaunt of Sir Floris." The volume thus composed is likely to win hearty appreciation from many who like to wander in the enchanted forests of poetry. In qualities of luxuriant grace and splendour of description Mr. Payne is eclipsed by few modern writers. In all metrical respect his verse is perfect. He has imagination, perception, and considerable lyrical power. There are in this book both promise and power.'—*The Sunday Times.*

The above volumes form, with the present work, a collection of Poems, intended to be called 'THE HOUSE OF DREAMS.'

In preparation, by the same Author,

1. TOURNESOL, AND OTHER ROMANCES IN VERSE.
2. SONGS OF THE GAEDHL.